The Learner's book

of short stories

DHANISTHA BHATTACHARJEE

BlueRose ONE.com
Stories Matter
NewDelhi • London

BLUEROSE PUBLISHERS
India | U.K.

BlueRose ONE.com
Stories Matter
NewDelhi • London

For permissions requests or inquiries regarding this publication, please contact:

BLUEROSE PUBLISHERS
www.BlueRoseONE.com
info@bluerosepublishers.com
+91 8882 898 898
+4407342408967

ISBN: 978-93-6261-195-6

Cover design: Tahira
Typesetting: Tanya Raj Upadhyay

First Edition: July 2024

Foreword

When my first story was accepted by a publishing house, it was a pretty decent start from then on. With the initial perks of being in the routine of writing and contemplating, it finally came to an end with the last one. To be frank and plain, it was all in the dreams of being a teen author that drove me to finish it. Not because it's unique, but because it just shows credibility. And I do like being recognised. Who doesn't? Every youngster does. Just to be clear about it, it's not that I do not like writing stories. I do like my own creations, and I do love stories, especially mystery, and fantasy ones. When you read this book, as a complete stranger with no intention of ever meeting me tell me how good or bad it is, it will be worthwhile enough for me. As for the content, I hope that I have done my utmost in pleasing the readers' senses with heart-touching and jaw-dropping moments in the short stories.

What one can effectively take and eventually benefit from the stories is how the power of one's imagination can convey greater and much deeper emotions than is possible through narration and preaching. I have imagined and written about it in the form of stories. "The Nightmarer" and "The Night with the Stranger" are my favorites, the ones that turned out the best for me. The rest is up to the readers to see whether they can love an anthology. Either way, I am grateful to you for picking up this book.

Preface

To start with, the first step is to really kick into that adrenaline needed to finish a project. I have been wanting to start this for so long—to become a young author and spread my love for reading and inventing to the world . It was the simple habit of racing through storybooks and textbooks that really connected me to the world of writing. I do not maintain a journal at this point, but planning to start with it with a view to habituate my writing as smoothly as my reading. Being a novice in the affairs of the world, doubts and regret are what come to my mind on thinking of starting something grand and out-of-my-comfort-zone. These include: What would it have been like if I had started earlier? How would I pull off all the steps single-handedly due to my introversion? How would I get over the fear of failure and rejection? Is it really that easy? All such doubts have arisen and will arise while I write this piece, short and simple. To the readers, it is a pleasure serving you all with my creation and I hope to make your read satisfying and your time worthwhile. When this book does come out and you get a chance to read this introduction, remember the innumerable doubts that had surfaced during the making of it, the number of days I have waited for this to take place and a belief that the 'the world is your oyster' and that you can make anything out of it, like clay, riddled with either the fruits of dedication, patience and innovation or of the shapelessness of regret, guilt and underperformance.

This book has ten short stories written over a rough period of one month or so, depending on how many days I have been disorganized enough not to continue. For starters, it's my first book, and I really hope to make a good impression with it. During the time which I had free after my exams, I planned to write it and publish it. None of the stories are really inter-connected, just the brainchild of my packed mind. No lay-out or character sketches. But good enough to keep you plodding till the last page.

Anyways, I do not plan to make this long enough to bore you. So, have fun reading.

Table of Contents

The one concerning Mr. Thomas Moor

From the diary entry of Mr. James Silow written by him before leaving for Warwick from the high-old Greggory fields of the West:

Of a strange nature is my complexion and whimsy while writing my experience in this entry in a way, as though I am leaving a part of my deep conscience in this blank piece of paper. I have been as much a part of the gossips and occasions practised and held in this sweet little town of West Burrow, where I have experienced every part of my sedentary lifestyle in for decades undocumented. In the outskirts of this town, the old and damp Greggory fields stretch far beyond the normal sight of vision. No one had a needle to pull out of that barren wasteland of a region, save for a few time-strained estates which stretched for a few acres over the coarse grass and had been occasionally honed by retired colonels and their geeky heirs. Other than that, it was left untouched by even the most playful and mischievous of cronies. The occasionally used estates were a certain luxury for the location, which did not have any other antic to attract pedestrians.

But I had a certain fancy to this dead place as it, for one, presented several opportunities which if exploited, could have very well brought me high acclaim in my field of occupation, i.e., real estate. In the years following my graduation, with the proper guidance given to me by my uncle Henry, who had acquainted me with the uneasiness of the estate holders in monetising their property, I had been able to effectively woo the retired professionals in appointing me as their agent. With the economy going downhill, something was needed urgently to give in profits while also becoming the ground for preserving capital. Consequently, with the acquaintance of finer individuals of my time who had come to these grounds on the pretext of being the estate shareholders, I had made a neat impression of my person upon their influence.

It was in keeping with the best of the waning glamour of the decade that I was capable of helping such individuals solidify their burning money on a fairground as the Greggory fields provided, situated close to the booming colonies. But as far as my intelligence can go into the uncanny fancies of the aristocrats and moguls with their deep inclination towards luxury and finery, it was yet in its infancy when making sense of the emotional capacity of man and the living. Of that insignificant part of the mind riddled with complexities and illusions drawn from rusty backgrounds and shadowy pasts, it was still unknown of and illogical in.

One Mr. Thomas Moor had me screaming after my logical conscience with his impressiveness of tone and apparent chivalry towards people of all ages and backgrounds in the field of small talk. I had the due grace of meeting this jolliest and most outstanding person, often referred to as an industry magnate by the cruel reporters.

That was what attracted my attention towards this crimson-haired and strong-jawed individual who had most of his public appearances in his iconic tweed suit and royal blue outfit, marking this young man as one of elegant taste and unmatchable charisma. Yet his youthful spirit and strong will to win an argument appeared to reason otherwise of his character.

It was on the evening of the farewell party of Sir Arthur Myers that I met this fine young man. He had garlanded his presence upon the occasion of being a distant partner of the retired gentleman in Shrubbery Villa, which beautifully sat upon the grassy lanes of the Greggorys. I was cordially welcomed and acquainted with the unknown visitor by Sir Arthur himself. Before I knew that he had some of the most distinguished accolades in his field of profession and was a successful person, I had thought of him as a thirty-something novice in the affairs of the world and having the most unrealistic of expectations to life and business. He had a boastful nature, whose intensity, for one, persuaded me to keep up the conversation of his business and other factors, fueling his speech with more excitement and thrill. This conversation, though, did not give the hint of any continuation or sequel. At Least, I thought so for what would a country dweller and business tycoon have so much to do with a small-town person, and on that matter, anything to do with this region?

My expectations from this person proved otherwise when just a week later I met him outside of my apartment in Farthington Square waving a golf stick at me. He was in a neat blue t-shirt and grey shorts, evidently in an athletic spirit. Although his informal clothing had me deceived of his intentions, it truly came to the surface when he expressed some willingness in buying an old country estate in the outskirts of the city. He may have thought that I was the right person for this task, as I had willfully explained my business of managing the properties riddled across the fields and had thus, having ridden its hot-headed owners of a burden. He had come in a yellow-coloured van which he parked near my building before we ventured out to explore the property.

I had a particular in mind, a rusty square-shaped villa most distant from the park gate which leads to the other establishments upon the Greggory fields. The villa had a wide porch in the front, bearing a swing and some dried-up plants in pots. It had been owned by a person named Shackford Millard, fairly younger in comparison to his neighbours and often out on long errands concerning his works of being a botanist. Mr. Moor had at once expressed the satisfaction of being its owner, before seeing the interior, which had given away to soot and the intolerable ravages brought upon by the seasons. The mahogany door opened into a great hall, a sitting area with stairs running along to the bedroom's upside on both sides. The curtains were dusty yet leathery giving a certain spooky state to the area by blocking off light. As I looked across the room and subsequently at my client, who had a certain determined look on his face, it reminded me of his eagerness to buy it immediately, not with the patience to seek out the best for sale. The pale look of satisfaction had run around all over his body, shown in the playful wink of the eye, a slow murmur of approval and subsequently coming out of his mouth as a "I like this place".

Either my extraordinary salesmanship had been at its best or this lean-faced chap might be showing the signs of being a fool in this era of finery and grandeur, giving way to his amateurish conscience. The Millards might not have been the first place I would seal a deal in when entering the complex world of estate-bundling, a term used by my uncle for the extravagant purchases of the idle classes. In that case, Mr. Moor might have been in the condition of a fish out of the water. My previous vivid experiences with these tycoons had rendered me somewhat of a biased view over the whole pack of industry giants, for I went on jabbering, "Why, yes, but it may please you to see others to have a better judgement, Mr. Moor."

His gaze shifted from the dusty marble of the floors to that of my suggestion, and with an uncomfortable expression he claimed, "No, this is perfect," Even to this day the placid expression on his face gives no clue to Luxor has been a crucial part of the memories of my profession. It has ceded well with me ever since that at a certain point of one's life, one needs a home rather than a house, to confide in and be nostalgic of all the grandeur that they had left behind. Yet this realisation had come at a remarkably young age for my client. To keep the verbal exchanges going at a convenient pace, I started, "If you like it as such, I can have a talk with Millard at Base, let him know of the interest," as my client sat patting the soft curtains looking out of the window occasionally. To my inquiry, he sprang up from his imagination and claimed that he had one condition upon which the purchase would be sealed: that he would stay at this house for the time of a month before paying the necessary amount.

I had been prepared for another of this man's fancy after my initial experience and gave my reply as a friendly nod, following which my client had the royalty to claim to pay for the due expenses to Millard and a commission to me. It had been one of those peculiar experiences with this man that I have grown to remember as hinting at cross paths with nobler sentiments, none that I have ever found among men of his class and prestige or will I ever come across in the years following my daily occupation.

My client had the ferocity of a bald eagle when jumping to conclusions and decisions and in acting upon them, he was as swift as a falcon, for only after our second meeting, I was acquainted with him only a day later. Walking casually through the coarse patch of dried-up vegetation upon the surroundings of his new lair, he waved at me with the anticipation of a child, who was promised a dream house as that which he expected me to make of that old mansion. I had in time talked to Mr. Millard and secured his approval on renting the house for a month and then while surveying for any reparations, the ecstatic voice of Moor shot me through the grass. He was willfully assisted by two boys who carried his luggage of two suitcases each. I was particularly thrilled at the thought that it was after a month that this tycoon would have to grace this rugged terrain every now and then.

The house was left as such on Moor's request who wished to make something grand of it. As a man bent on obtaining customer satisfaction, it had been my regular from then on to check up on this new tenant and resident on whether the new conditions had ceded him well. Only a good few days had passed after that when every local tongue had the name of this charming persona in their conversation. The people in my town had been reclusive to the idle classes and hardly crossed the park gate of the fields, not because they had a bone to pick from these wealthy people but simply to say that they did not relate anything with them. But the young royal of a friendly nature broke even this streak of his class. Once I had seen him boasting to the old milkman how he had punched a gorilla while on a business venture to the South, and on another day getting playful with the neighbourhood chickens and their soulful young owners. It was weird and sweet, idle and thoughtful, but none the different work for his person and character. Often, I assisted him on his morning and evening walks to the town where he made sure to have the goodwill of every single person, as in greeting them and taking note of their presence. During one of these times, we shared some of the facts of our daily life, he being boastful about his ventures and takeovers as though it had not yet been normal for him to have these occasional bursts of success. I had been somewhat restrictive till then having solidified my manner of action among foreigners and clients. But he had proved an exception.

His lively nature had given me the impression that it was something about his childhood that shaped his habits, but I could not be more deceived. Two weeks in he had set up a reputation of being the liveliest host and foreigner of West burrow. Yet the purpose of my defining him is to have you readers understand that often the face of man, such as it is, convey an entirely different scenario than that which surrounds common sense. I witnessed this after the gentleman had been on my friendly list of clients. On the third week of his stay, I had the leisure of visiting him in person at his lair. There in the corner of the hall, tucked comfortably into a ball was he waiting for me to begin the conversation. He was fairly normal as ever but none the more straightforward, as it had been. I deduced that it was something concerning his business or personal life which was still unknown to me. His countenance had the subtle expression of being influenced by a recent event or situation. It was draining his energy and he may have needed some company. For much of our conversations, it was either his successful ventures or future endeavours that he talked about, none concerning his personal life. From the time that I saw those glittering eyeballs of his seeing more than being shown, his hunched shoulders signalling the presence of something pinning him to exhaustion, he felt the direst need to share it.

"Have you seen the newspaper?" he mused dryly as if talking to his mind. Confused, I replied, "No, why?"

"Never mind, they do not show anything valuable," a sign of distaste had settled on his brows towards which he had some personal hatred.

I went on with it but seeing him bear a rare expression of anxiety, I went over to his side and patting his shoulder with my palm, I replied, "What's the matter with you?", to which he looked at me with the same distrustful eyes and angst.

"You don't know anything about me, do you?" his query was genuine and undisputed for behind all his unrequited energy and brilliance, there was a child inside him waiting among the darkness to explain his condition, if only the world were not busy labelling him for what he does rather than what he is. It was never in the papers or in the media, anything which concerned his health and prosperity (and, mind you, I do not mean external prosperity). All these thoughts had not been in my mind at that time, for my client had maintained such a poker face that I could not deduce anything from that. To further extend my knowledge about the matter, I said, "Maybe not well enough, I do not know what it is that pains you." I continued, "Tell me, Tom. What is it?"

He needed no more encouragement to withhold, for after this he went on, "All right, it is what it is. I would not force you to keep it to yourself," he coughed a good deal before starting,

"You know, James, I was an orphan living with a farmer on a farm, like this. I did not know when I was born or that my parents were dead. But that farmer who told me to have discovered me in the woods told me that they were dead. I was pretty timid and shy since childhood, so I read alone, ate alone in a barn, and slept alone staring at the night sky riddled with specks of light. One day, a family came into the farm, maybe they had their car run down or something. I served them with bread and tea, securing them to a place in the barn. At night, while sitting by a post and staring mindlessly at the stars, I saw the girl looking at me from the barn gate. I inquired and she replied that she could not sleep in the heat and felt bored. To lighten the moment, I asked whether she wanted to watch the stars to which she gladly sat beside me without saying anything. She was a blabber-mouth, for one as she kept on telling me about her imaginary household. It was pretty childish, yet I did not give into it but kept listening. At last, she asked me whether I had any friends or not, I replied in the negative and looked up. You know what happened after that?", Sate asked stolidly not expecting a reply, for he went on immediately, "She ran up to the barn and brought her little purse back from which she took out a blue bracelet, the one made from those squared-shaped beads. She gave it to me saying, "Will you be my friend?", I was too awe-struck to reply but gazed at the bracelet in which a word was printed on each block. Together, they spelt, "HILDA" With that my client sat in amusement and stared blankly towards the ceiling, I intervened, "Is that the ending?"

"No, it was the beginning. Something had influenced me; it may be friendship or a sense of belonging somewhere hopeful. But I was ten and dumb, so I kept that bracelet and assured the girl with a friendly smile. It was all I saw of her for the next decade to follow. But that night had changed something in me for the better, I guess. I kept on with my routine as it was up to the age of sixteen, when that farmer sent me to the nearby town, to collect some items. It was the nearest that I had been to scores of people and, for one, it thrilled me, so I decided to stay. A job at a nearby bakery was all that I needed to survive in that place. It steamed in me a desire to shine, for the time. I still saw fewer faces but maybe I do not like to talk about that,"

"Moor, what is the point" I asked him grayly, seeking an answer for his contradictory behaviour. The man had changed paler by this, his throat throbbed and that sprain of exhaustion surrounded him, for he did not want to express any further, yet that grueling burden of the past surpassed this discomfort, and he coarsely replied,

"Well, I worked hard and hard, and then some wise gentleman noticed me one day. He was not old but he understood my state and potential. I read and wrote pretty well at that age. Old habit, I guess. I flourished from then on, but......." he halted for the recollection or maybe for the realisation, whatever it was, but it poked him deeply,

"Well, Tom, this is important that my first objective was to find Hilda before I even came into that town. I wanted to grow to be able to find her. And I did see her on a boat while I was on a voyage to the Marin Bay. About a decade later or so. The same playful eyes and a bushy bun, and dressed the same,"

"Well, what did you do?" I queried. Again, a deep emotion changed his contours, sucking away all the joy that this nostalgia had bestowed on him and he only gave me a vague expression with the word, "Nothing" on it.

That was the second to last conversation I had with him, much more thought-provoking and solemn than the rest of it which had been the base of my understanding for this man's character. I was on square one with this part, for before that he had been nothing less than free-spirited and merry. I wanted an explanation for his behaviour, but seeing his dreamy eyes sinking back to his queer past, I had nothing more to say. It was certainly not the last though, that I saw of him. An unplanned get-together planned our last meet-up, and it was hosted by none other than Thomas Moor himself, down in his villa on the

Greggory fields. The day following the above conversation, I woke up quite early for a walk, for my mind did not spare me from replaying the conversation again and again in hopes of finding an answer; I had not been so unprofessional before as I was in this scenario. Anyways, a slight view towards the fields while I was passing them, and I saw Tom standing against a post evidently in conversation with Mr. Gollocks, his neighbour. He bore a casual expression of unknowingness as if the tides never turned against him and he had not been halted in his joy by some news.

Till the time which I have narrated, Tom had spent a good twenty-five days in that villa, and his month of rest was ending. He had to join his industrial forces in the north, which he had handed over to his secretary, Ruffles, as I came to know of it. It was evidently for business reasons that the meet-up was conducted, for many new faces blended into that shimmering night of thrill. I had to be there for a warm invitation had been spread throughout the neighbourhood for the same, encouraging everyone to be a part of the entourage's joy. And was it a big go-to for the town's folk? Children and women dressed in their best outfits adorned the dry land, adults too maintaining their level of exposure to the foreigners who came in piles and groups from the north through the fanciest of cruises and in the shiniest of attires. While the children sprinted around the scrub vegetation in circles, through the bumpy crossways and shadowy boulders, scores of groups had formed in clusters, all around the villa, seeking the company of the host of the night, who was evidently in one of the rooms of the building. No company had seen him till then and my presence was more as a friend rather than as an agent. These new folks had a certain level of finesse in their habits, quite the professional tone for me. I had the grace of meeting one of them, a middle-aged clerk who seemed to have gotten into the best of the company, for he had acquired a certain speech, perfected into something of a monologue, praising his organisation for all it is. I had not gotten a thing of it before I was approached by a burly figure, bald and limping towards me with a note in one hand. It was Mr. Ruffles and I was unaware of it. For all that I could recollect of his behaviour, he had streamed at me with an inquiry, "Are you Mr. Silow?". My affirmation had an impressive expression upon his person and he declared authoritatively, "Mr. Moor desires to speak to you,"

"Where is he?" my curiosity replied, to which I was escorted by this gentleman into the house, through the stairs and near the bedroom door, whose light streamed through the gap between the door and the floor. Leaving me to my wits, the secretary disappeared from sight. For my conscience, my client was getting more mysterious by the day. Why was it that he needed to avail the services of his assistant to call me? Was it because of our previous conversation? None of these questions deserved to remain unanswered so I opened the door in such hopes, only to find its bearer spread into an armchair in his iconic tweed suit. His elbows rested on his thighs and the end of one hand supported his grief-stricken state so that I could not see his face which stared at the dusty marble between his booted feet. His other hand which rested on his other thigh had a letter secured, probably opened and read by the person. Whatever it had been, it was surely in contrast to the general atmosphere which our surroundings bore that night. But the host was still quiet as a predator, not able to come out of whatever situation the day had presented. I meekly inquired, "Are you fine?", it did not interest his character so I called out to him again, only to be ignored. But he did heed my concern after I turned towards the door, in a voice which I never had connected with this person, until then. In a coarse and grave tone, he said, "She died, James,"

"Hilda?" I recollected her name from our previous conversation with the same surprise and despondence as the host had, "What happened?"

"Tuberculosis, inflicted from that same crew in which I had last seen her. She had been fighting it for months, and.................." his tone gave way to the mental agony that he was in.

"And?" I interfered.

"....I was not there because.......I chose this." he claimed while hinting at the vast Luxor of the hall which had been his sole reason of not achieving what he wanted. Once again, I was in a pickle with this, and the more I tried to reason with him about it, nothing seemed to cross my mind which could make sense of it all. It was so frustrating so I straight-up attempted for an answer, "I am sorry, Tom for whatever it is you are facing, but you have to stop being so mysterious," I paused to look into the man's eyes which were still staring at the marble floor. Standing over his head, I gently massaged his shoulder before continuing, "If you want me to be of some help, just make a clean breast of everything, will you?"

At this remark, he looked up a me from his palms, his eyes were red and watery bearing a symphony of agony and anger and he replied, "You know why I did not go on that boat in Martin Bay?.............Because I had a bunch of people aboard, my directors, colleagues, and other people more professional than me,somehow knew more thane of what I wanted.It all looked enlightening. So, I stopped over to finish that deal. It all went booming from then on, but......" he paused for a time with a more solemn gaze at me and then said, "I lost everything that I had that day.....in exchange.......I got this," his direction was towards the gaudy crowd of professionals and entrepreneurs warming the surroundings of his lawn with their laughter and cheer, downside. Through the curtains, the glamour of that decade combined into a get-together and farewell was coming to life in the dead of the night. My client looked distastefully at the crowd from the slit, with an occasional hurtful glance at me. The matter was now before me and I had no clue how to be of assistance to this ailing man who had just lost what he wanted for so long, friendship and companionship. Standing in the light of the burning candle, I could only think of that time when I had seen him all dressed up in royal blue at the farewell party, all that time bearing the fundamental demeanour of royalty, when inside it was all grey and bleak.

It was past midnight when he returned to his senses while having me by his side, as confused as a parrot, and the last I heard from his voice was, "James, it may be all confusing to you having a client crying for something that never could have happened,"

I heard a scream inside of me, forcing me to say these words, the only ones I was able to make sense of, "You just wanted to be there for her. It is not a complex analogy, just..emotion." I had no more to speak about and I turned to leave from the room which had turned darker......with the light of the candle ready to give up at any moment. It was a surprise for me to hear anything from my client but I heard this last words reaching me,

"If life were as easy as giving bracelets..............." it was incomplete but yet only that creasy part I needed to draw up the character of my client, cloudy and vague.

And thus, had our acquaintance ended in the night of the 31st and it evidently was the last I saw of Thomas Moor, the last that I ever wished to not see. Right from the meetup at the farewell to our evident parting at his villa, all the sights and antics of this man have astounded me ever since. While I try to sketch his persona in words in this entry, many incidents concerning his disappearance after that party on the 31st have occurred in and around. I have been interviewed relentlessly by such reporters seeking his whereabouts to where he might be and from one of them, an ambitious one, I found out that Mr. Henry Atticher had been the man in fueling his desires from the time when he found him in the town's bakery. I awed at this coincidence brooding over whether all of Tom's sufferings had come to surface only because my uncle had noticed him, and helped him.

Over a certain point in my life, where I am old and unmarried, idling in the neighbourhood as the realtor in me had been slumbering for long, I came to realise that my ex-client was never made for a business life, that his charm had been at play to attract people who he thought were his guides. In all of those decisions where he chose to obey, he also chose how his life would be, unknowingly. He went out to look for friends but got partners and assistants. That night was his last straw to ending this streak, and he chose so. Not that I will ever know of his whereabouts, but it is clear that he is somewhere less scary. As to the house, it went to charity for all I know. If only I could ever believe in being in a similar pickle as he was in, I would have had more peace and more affection towards his class.......................

......And more sleep.Instead of writing this.

All in the woods

Little Jim walked speedily around the light post near the entrance of his primary school from where big crowds of schoolchildren were beginning to disperse in twos or threes along the muddy road in front of their school. The boy looked restlessly towards the crowd in search of a familiar face, all to no avail.

"Jim!" called a familiar voice from among the disbanding crowd, a shrewd countenance bearing a look of exuberance upon its lips.

"Greg, here, what is it?" he looked exhaustingly at his friend with the annoyance of having been abandoned.

"I got your pencil back, here, look..." Greg remarked with a certain ecstasy before placing a dull-coloured pencil on Jim's palm for him to observe. It had grown shorter and had stealthier bite marks near the graphite point . That, along with the solemn covering of that shady-coloured body , amounted to no satisfaction on the part of the tan-coloured and hot-headed boy.

"It does look good, Greg," Jim said unenthusiastically.

"Tim had it, for all I know," Greg continued, noticing that his recent discovery had not favored his friend, who stood steaming with annoyance near the light post. So, with the boastfulness of a child who had not yet been exposed to the world, he spoke out".

"Jim, will you please go with me to Cunnin' side, please...." he asked meekly.

"Why do you want to go to scary places? I do not plan to do so." Jim replied in a mix of annoyance and subtlety.

"It's just......."Greg had not formed a reason for going into that strange hovel of a settlement where abandoned establishments lay rotting in the scarce sunlight. Before he could counter his argument, an authoritative voice reached them, calling 'Greggory' in a subtle rhythm. Greg went on with his mother through the road, leaving Jim buzzing furiously near the post, even as the sun was beginning to drive into a slumber for the day. "He forgot!" Jim mused as if in conversation with the wind blowing noisily over the dry figs and fallen leaves. The last rays of the sun lit the pathways as Jim began to trudge along the road, gnashing his jaws. "Fine! I'll do it alone" he shouted into the windy atmosphere and the silence ignited him to speed up his tread. Walking away from the school, he heard the thin whining of the bluejay, slowly getting into its nightly routine. The dark and desolate streets gave him a tingling sensation but he persevered through this, finally stopping before a clearing which got into a narrow pathway. The icing on the cake was that the broad canopy of trees, possessing long trunks and deep roots scarcely gave in to the fury of the winds, hence covering the path and sparing no light to cross it. For these reasons, it made a pretty spooky but nonetheless familiar stride which brought the pedestrians into the broader and crowdier area of the town. It was the dread of his solo walk that numbed his bravado of knowing every nook and corner of his mighty town, Willsbury. Jim stood poised before the dark tunnel of a path or rather frozen at the thought of having to journey through it alone. He had crossed it before many times but not without walking timidly behind his brother, who having the knack of being a supportive big brother, had the understanding to let him do so. But not today as it seemed, resulting in Jim juggling between the thoughts of consequences and repercussions. Some scrawny-eyed idlers had the daring to spread a rumour about it: that the twisted tentacles like branches of the oldest trees housed spirits of witches and crows, who did not take a moment's breath to feed upon the souls of the ignorant. Smart or not, he quickly gave in to this rumour.

Then something sprang up from his conscience.

'Out of sight, out of mind,' was today's proverb for the week, he remembered.

Without wasting a second, Jim ran furiously through the darkness with a closed pair of eyes. The distance between both sides of the path was large enough to have him scurry through it without a tree to interfere. In about a minute, he had reached the other side of the tunnel panting heavily before a broader intersection of the path. On his way homeward, as the little schoolboy trudged wistfully through the lit road, the jolly babel of Mr. Willis, sporting on the green before his two-roomed home caught his attention.

Seeing his friendly neighbour, Jim heaved a sigh of relief at having made it home. And with a childish vengeance, he thought of teaching a lesson to whom he owed a breath or two. If I were to put the character of Tommy Wincock in a word, the big brother of Jim, it would be excellent at best and authoritative at worst. In his excellency, he had been a strong pillar of support for his younger brother. Taking after his father, he was known to inculcate in Jim the braver qualities of men in ways that seeps into the daily routine, in ways such that a picky and clingy kid can easily bear with without knowing. The best way to do so is by making those tasks stringent as Mr. Willis puts it in his humorous tone when Jay Wincock went into thin air, it was in the trunks of his elder son that he did rest. Thus, when Tommy heard the bitter the footsteps of his brother echoed through the halls of their home. A satisfied smile played on Tommy's lips as he lay sprawled on his bed, engrossed in a sports magazine. The sound grew louder, transforming into angry stomps that rattled the pictures on the wall. Finally, the bedroom door swung open with a bang. Tommy looked up to see his brother, Jim, radiating childish rage and angst. "What is it, little brother?" Tommy asked pleasantly, never taking his eyes off the magazine. "You left me!" It was more of a question rather than a reply to his brother that poured out of Jim's lips.

"Have I? No, I didn't go,"

"Why didn't you pick me up?"

"I thought you could come on your own. It's time you do so." "I do not like the forest. You know that"

"Jim, you have to conquer that fear," Tommy said dismissively. "There's nothing to be afraid of."

"Why did you leave me?" Jim asked earnestly seeking an answer, his inquisitiveness booming with the validation of his brother's poker and no-care face.

"You came on your own, didn't you?" Tommy pointed out, this time looking right into the twinkling eyes of Jim, who was not at a point to agree with his brother but gave in to his reason with a nod. He had crossed the clearing alone. But it was not that he was all daring and friendly with the atmosphere. It was more fear, less rage that drove him to do what he did.

Presently, Tommy sat up and urged his brother to come close, to which he obliged due to their endearing bond. He curled his arm around Jim and said,

"You are six. You know what I used to do when I was six?" Jim replied with a grin of un- surety and said," You taught the chickens how to lay eggs and dictate their chicks?"

"Umm...not exactly. I ventured into the forest at the Tesley's, the one connected with the clearing. I met a stranger there, living in the woods, all bushy mustache and ragged apparel. But he was friendly and kind and funny. And a great showman."

"Showman?"

"He told me about the forest and also a perfect way to crack nuts." "Is this a secret?"

"I told Dad when he disappeared." "Who, the showman?"

"Into thin air. I never went there again. Anyway, what I am saying is that it might be that what you are scared of is not the woods but the silence and darkness that comes with it. If you do explore it, I am sure it will be a friendly ride."

"So, I have to go to the woods now because of you?"

"No, you don't. Only when you want to." Tommy replied with a humorous grin, and offering him his teenage wisdom, he stood up and went out. Jim was left to his wits. He had not yet the desire to explore the forest but somehow his nagging brother had sparked in him the desire to opt for a reason.

He did stumble upon it the next day at school when while gobbling up his share of cereals at breakfast, he witnessed the dreadful expression of his friend, Greg streaming at him from the other side. The child had a weary look upon his countenance mixed with horror and trauma, as though something regarding his nightmares concerning the Cunnin' side had come true and upon him. Jim looked sideways at any possible bullies and finding none asked Greg," Hey, why are you staring at me?"

"You know I heard something?" Greg replied blatantly "Where?"

"Cunnin' side,"

"You went there alone?"

"I wanted to find my pouch up there."

"Why did you go alone? How did you lose your pouch up there?" Jim asked sternly.

Greg looked up at him from his bowl embarrassingly as though there was no other choice for him to choose from, and then bowed his head. He went on," I heard someone cough and swear furiously,"

"Just that?"

"No, he was cutting something," "You saw a woodcutter?"

"No, Jim............it was not a woodcutter!"

"What was it then?"

"I.........don't know, I had fainted and I think he caught me,"

"And you're scared now?"

"He was hairy and rough......and an axe was there. Then he left me." "Did you tell anyone about it?"

"You, only. What do you think about it..." "Hairy...kind...was he bulky?"

"I don't know, but he had caught me." "To help you...."

Jim had stopped eating and was now thinking upon this knowledge, as it had struck him hard, now that his friend insisted. His curiosity had risen about the mystery man. Kind and hairy-two qualities he had heard Tommy speak about a man who existed a decade ago. Were they the same person or a doppelganger of some sort? Whatever it was, it was eating his cereal. "Did you see him?" he asked at last to which Greg was uncertain and unsure of the person being even a no-stranger. It sparked his desire all the more but this time, he knew where to satiate it.

The jungle was a dense-grown pack of deciduous and tropical vegetation. The least-cared for and hence the most flourishing of all packs. These further solidify its status of being an inhospitable hub, with entangled bamboo and branches spreading far and ahead. Some kind mister had in some century taken the burden of taking out a clearing through it, leaving the nightmarish tinge of darkness to the pedestrians' fancy. An eerily bordered one at that, it was not tiresome for mischief to take place about this rumoured place or weirdly-set trips of explorations as our little Jim was about to take to his mind.

"An inhospitable hub..." he had heard his teacher say.

As he stood before the line of abyssal silence, it struck him that it was not so much the horror of it all that dreaded him about this trip but that he did find it unwelcoming and boring so much so that it became unsettling for him. Now as he stood sternly, the silence seemed to enchant him and welcome him into a mystery to be solved.

It was all exciting for his liking and so he took his flight. A little among the towering trees and he saw a stamped part of the grass made into a little track for travel. He followed the smoothness of the track, further into the jungle eventually stumbling upon a tree in the middle not without a visible hint.

"What crook is that!" He was eyeing an arrow mark of a direction towards the left. It did not take him long to make up his mind about continuing left, and he did so. All along this time, he was accompanied by varied combinations of trees, crooked, bent, joined at the stem, stunted growth, each quirkier than the preceding. The world seemed to shrink into another woodland with barky residents and hairy inhabitants. By the time that Jim's exuberance gave way, the ground had gone drier and the surroundings rougher. The fresh greenery of the branches above him left a speck of blueness uncovered. Jim stared at the blue dot, unaware of his next move, until the childish side of his genius spoke up, “Hello!”

His voice echoed through the silence of the woods. Jim shouted, “Is anyone there? Mister hairy person?!!” Again, the curious jangle of speech travelled through the woods, taking after the frightening appeal of songbirds and squirrels that followed it. But it wasn’t to go unnoticed in any way by the mystery man.

Jim heard a constant knocking sound after that, specific to a particular direction, presumably the left. He heard it and went rogue, but as the sound faltered and lessened it was a soothing silence. As to the sound’s origin, its bearer had a certain knack for surprises and peek-a-boo shows. So, when Jim took to leaving the place, he turned only to witness the built and broad musculature of the hairy man in front of him, a bushy beard, greyish scalp evidently covered in age-hold whiskers with an axe possessed in one hand. Quite a terrifying spectacle for a child, but somehow Jim was all at ease with that. He had, in fact, ignored all the other features but looked straight into the eyes, almond-ish and foreboding calm and tranquility in its pupils, proof of its kindness.

“Eyes are the image of one’s soul,” another fact he had read somewhere. “Hello! Who are you?”

“I live here.” “Here, where?”

“In the woods, over there” He pointed with his axe in the direction of the sound.

“Have you been living here for long? Because I think you might know my brother, Tommy,"

"I don't think so." The stranger replied after some thought and with conviction.

"Hmmm....you don't.......then you are someone else. Do you know the person who lived here, wherever, before you?"

"I don't............Look, I think you shouldn't be here at this hour" the stranger replied in an authoritative tone, presuming the character of a wayfarer rather than a mystery man.

"I wanted to find out about you because Tommy said do you know

how to crack nuts or something more thrilling?"

The stranger was growing more impatient by the minute as Jim's aspirations and vocals grew. It was evident that he wasn't used to company and the child's presence was all the more worrisome.

The man said," Did you come here on your own?" "Yes!" came the reply in excitement.

"Ok, if you go for now, I will meet you soon" "Really, do you promise?"

"I do."

"Will you teach me your methods?"

"What.......fine I will what I know." the man said assuringly.

Jim had grown more ambitious, unaware that the day had turned into a quieter evening, sparking the stranger's worry." What is your name?" he asked.

"Jim!"

"Ok, Jim, you mustn't be here in the evening. We will keep our conversation on some other day at a reasonable hour. You go for now."

"Should I come tomorrow? It's a holiday." "Uh, what about after that?"

"No, I do want to finish it quick. Please mister hairy man, I know you are kind."

"Ok, fine. Now you go." "Ok, sleep tight, Mister."

And thus, went the conversation between these two, Jim being overly expectant and the stranger being a certain bit skeptical, unaware that it was to follow a revelation.

For his age, Jim was cautious and a bit more conscious than his counterparts. When he decided to find the hairy stranger in the woods, he had also pledged to conceal the identity of him, if he were to be his friend. Of course, he thought that someone who likes living alone must also, be equally reluctant towards public attention. If Jim were to tell Greg about the coughing stranger, it would certainly be cruel to their friendship, then no learning and cracking nuts. So, he discreetly maintained his cool while going home, bearing a poker identity along the whole trip. He was so mild and confident about it that no rounds of interrogation were inflicted on him, nor was he subjected to the cheery and knowing glances of his big brother. All went peacefully that night which was to continue into an adventurous rendezvous for the heart of Jim the next morning.

And boy did it do for him, when on the bright morning; Jim woke up early to prepare himself for the meet-up. Brushing his teeth and doing his hair into a cadet-like style, he packed some items in his backpack, mainly a rope, some nuts, and a book, which he had found lying near Tommy's desk. After the morning chores of the house was followed, Jim declared to his mother that he would be out with Greg for the day, helping him in finding his pouch near Cunnin' side. Surely reluctant at first, Ms. Wincock later gave in to her son's persuasion, unaware of his endeavours.

Jim went happily through the same route into the slimy jungle, much more familiar with the environment, now that he had a purpose. Reaching the same spot, to his delight, he found the hairy gentleman, leaning against a stunted tree, waiting with a mix of surprise and grudging acceptance. "Good morning, Mister."

"Did you tell anyone?"

"Oh no, I did not want to scare you out. I want to be your friend."

"And why is it so?" the questioning glances of the man were cast upon Jim.

"Greg said you were kind." "And? "

"And I want to be your friend."

The man had grown a subtler expression of defeat over his countenance, saying," Ok, you just want to be my friend, then?"

"Yes, I want to learn to crack nuts the easy way." "I don't like nuts."

"Then you can teach me to say," Jim said enthusiastically while peering at the rusted axe of the stranger.

“It's not for kids to mess with,”

“You are just like my brother, you know, then you tell me what it is, you know?”

The man looked around with a puzzled air for some time before heaving an expression of profound joy on his wrinkly skin.” How about this!” he boomed before jumping into a frenzy. Grabbing the slim branch of a tree, no higher from the ground than him and taking it as a support, he swung and caught hold of the bark, before climbing at full throttle up to the highest branch. His hands holding onto the grooves and bite marks on the bark aided him in this conquest, but it was all the more difficult and unimaginable for Jim who stood in awe and witnessed the man’s speed at the task.

“Jim!” the man called the bewildered boy from the highest point of the tree.

“Will you teach Me?” Jim replied.

His remark was met by a knowing glance from the climber. For the next hour that they spent together, Jim was engrossed in the task beforehand. He was impressed at the boy’s focus and the two had a time mastering the student-teacher relationship. Jim listened to the man talking about the grip of his hand and how to enhance it by holding the bark in a certain way. With the legs, he was instructed to push it into the bark of the tree, maintaining balance and being confident. Overall, it was a mighty simple and easy task but to Jim, it meant learning and adventure. In three-quarters of an hour, he was waving gleefully towards his teacher from a bulky branch of a taller tree.” That was good!” Jim said while climbing down.

"You learned fast. Pretty good for your age." "You taught well. Pretty good for you."

"Jim, it's nearly afternoon, you must be home for lunch"

"Ya, ok, I gave an excuse to Mom that I am helping Greg in finding his pouch on Cunnin's side. It's mighty solid. You know that place after Maggie's thrift center. All shabby and wreckage."

"I do know it," the man remarked with a subtle tone.

"By the way, are we meeting again?" Jim asked hopefully. "Asking me or telling me?"

"Why, you don't know anything except climbing?"

"Axing and shaving my hair. Again, you're too young for that."

"How about bird-calling?"

"I don't know why that is necessary."

"That is to tame birds. Anyways, how do you make food?"

"Why are you asking so much?" the man inquired with a hurried air. The unease was gaining momentum in his throat as the sun came upon them," You should go now."

"Should I? Not before you tell me about your next subject." "Ok, how about we decide on our next meeting?" "Here, no. Tomorrow."

"With a good excuse."

"Wait, mister. I have something for you." Jim said before taking out the book from his backpack, "It is for you to read at your leisure, when you are free. I am sure you can read."

"You didn't have to do that, but thank you." the man replied with a thin tone as if touched by the gesture. It all thus, came to a halt for the day as they bid farewell, Jim being more delighted at having found a mysterious friend. As the wind of the evening swept the sweat from the boy's face, the footsteps of this tiny adventurer springing off homewards. The cycle of their camaraderie had begun with the book.

It was to go daily from then on like this. Every time after school, Jim would trudge gleefully towards the tunnel and make for his tread through the forest to meet his friend who had begun to keep well with him. He didn't have much to teach except the climbing and axing. For some, Jim stared at him and saw the cut stems neatly and vigorously while talking about school. On days when all learning was finished, Jim would talk about his family, about his brother busy being his father, his mother working hard to make up for the absence of his father, his father not being there and all other stuff. The stranger could only nod and listen to the boy who had found a friend in him and was too sweet-hearted to stop the exchange. One day when Jim realised that he had called the person 'Mister' or 'hairy dude' for a long, he asked him his name. The stranger was visibly surprised at the suddenness of this, but after reverting to his composed behaviour replied, "Jerry".

Jim liked the name and said that it was the name he gave to a friendly squirrel once when he had found him in his backyard, "It is a good name. I wish I had asked for it sooner." The boy regretfully revealed and the day ended with a slight revelation.

Now, if I have talked about this pair's adventures for long, let us revert for a second to the household.......meaning Tommy. He was as sure as a wolf that something was up with his little brother. He had been way too jolly lately, much in contrast with his hot-headedness, and had been going on about his day in school mostly alone, not that it was too out of his character but that it looked suspicious. He was fine, though, with it as long as Jim went about his day happily, sinking in his heart whatever there was to hide. Until he had found out that his airman journal was gone. And the lucidity with which Jim vouched for the missing journal tipped Tommy off that there was a secret lying somewhere in Jim's tricky little brain. One sunny morning while Jim stared wistfully at the sky, exhausted from his chores, Tommy approached him and said," Why, Jimmy, is something wrong with your mind?"

"Why do you say so?"

"Well, as the matter goes, you do not fear the tunnel anymore." "Why, yes. Do you want me to fear it again? So that you can walk with me." "It's not so. But I presume you have something up your sleeves that you don't like to talk about."

"And why do you say so?"

"Don't try to be a mystery. I can read you through." Tommy smirked. He was surely confident of knowing his brother, the one whom he had been dictating about rules and work for so long that he could spot a whisker different in him, and he said, "I know you like mysteries. But keep out of trouble. You know the last time it went so, I had to pull you out of a tree."

"It won't happen again. I know how to climb." "Really, and how do you know that?"

"A friend taught me."

"I am sure he is not in kindergarten." "Oh, he is older than you."

"Don't you know what mom told you about strangers?"

"We are not strangers, though. I tell him about my day and he listens while chopping wood."

"A woodsman?"

"Yes, it is so. Just like you,"

"Jim, please keep your way out from strangers as such. And it's not the same. My father knew the truth and you don't end your time being all but you."

"Why do you poke me every time?"

"It's only for the sake of warning you. Dad did the same thing to me."

"At least stop being my father sometime," Jim said furiously and before Tommy could utter another word, he ran off into the courtyard and by jumping over the fence, out of his house. It was evident that he was planning on going near the woods. It was not new to him; the occasional poking around had been endured since he had learned to run and cycle. He could not give more thought to the past with his brother as he was busy venting it out on the ground. He sprinted ahead. Tom's words followed him. To meet Jerry and vent this new-grown anger on him inculcated by his brother. Speeding through the dry, brown leaves that crunched under his feet , he made for the spot through the crooked trees, the way of which he had skillfully marked with tape on the bark. He stopped at that spot among the trees, and threw his lungs out for Jerry, only to not have a blue Jay cry in protest. It was sultry and still in the afternoon, no crows in sight, nor no axing. Jim was growing impatient by the second.

Something concerning Tommy's words had never failed to boil his blood, whether it was something regarding his coarse-old tone of wisdom or of the fact that he always succeeded in inserting reminders of Dad. Why did he have to talk about the person Jim had never met or talked with? He would rather talk about Jerry or the hungry ailing cockatoo in the nest. Maybe it was that which reminded Jim of not knowing something of his life. Something of a mystery he had failed to solve. And he does hate leaving a mystery unsolved; It was this urge that emboldened him to befriend Jerry.

"Jerry!" he shouted at the top of his lungs for him, as though venting his anger with every shout. Something of his childish innocence and patience had given way to fury and angst. It remained as such, unheard of, for a long time. His patience turned into fury and gradually transformed into dejection and disappointment. Seeing a half-crooked tree near him, he climbed with the impatience of a fourteen-year-old and went as far as the slimmest, and highest branch. Having secured his hold over the stem, he sat on the branch, staring into oblivion, into nothingness and at the half-cut stem of a forlorn tree. It reminded him of Jerry, who had not heard his call. Maybe he was taking an afternoon nap, Jim thought and he visualised him sleeping soundly on a lice-infested sheet spread over a stuff of cotton in a wooden cottage, far up in the north, but nearer to the Cunnin' side. He was so engrossed in his thought that picturing the snoring face of the woodsman lured him to close his eyes. It was no ordinary as he was falling asleep.

When he did open his eyes, it was nothing like the branch of the tree he had been on. It was a fluffy mattress on which he rested, covered by a thin sheet, and instead of the half-cut stem, he could see a burning candle giving out a lovely glow standing over the cupboard. But the little boy had yet to realise that the mattress on which he slept were not his, the candle which he was eyeing were not set by his mother and the tall, broad-shouldered man which came in through the half-opened door in front of him was not the bulky man he had met in the woods, except that it was still Jerry. Jim could only come out of his slumber once the man asked, "You wake up?"

"Uh, what Jerry? Is it you?"

"Yes, it is I."

"What, you look different."

"Did you realise that you had fallen asleep on the tree branch, about twice your height from the ground?"

"The first one I do. You rescued me?" "I brought you to a comfier place." "Here, is it your home?"

"Yes, it is. Since I don't know your address, I had to bring you here. You have a deep slumber."

"Jerry, why didn't you wake me up?"

"It's four in the morning, now. I got you up at eight."

"It must be the medicine that my mother gave me for the wound." "Jim, tell me your address, I will take you home

"It's late, I will go alone wait, why do you look different?"

"I shaved today."

"Is this your cottage?" "This is my home. Rented."

"I read the daily newspaper also." "Pretty modern for you."

"Listen.......I need to tell you a thing or two." Jerry announced submissively, before standing up and going near the old cupboard that stood near the door." It is now time........." he began in a low tone," that I go back."

"Where?" Jim asked confidently. "To Wencrow, now."

"Never heard about it. Is it your home?"

"Yes, and not here. So, I have to move away now, Jim" his voice had begun to dwindle.

"So, you are disappear......" Jim continued quietly beginning to take account of the situation.

"I'm not because I am telling you that. I'm not abandoning you, Jim." "You are now. Everyone does so."

"Don't be ridiculous, Jim. I want you to remember me as a friend, now and again. And it won't hurt you to share those feelings with your brother......if it's required."

“No, it’s not. Why does he have to do anything with this? He just bosses me around every time.”

The man had begun to show an expression of guilt and defeat upon his countenance which blended well with the wrinkles on his temple. He had nothing more to argue for but on a last resort, he continued,” This is the last thing we will talk about today..................... it’s important that you remember it.” his voice complemented the solemn sight of his eyes that began,” It’s never too late to make amends. But there’s a time to do so and if it just glides off, there’s........................ nothing much we can amend then.”

The boy sat on the bed with a puzzled expression on his face and stared suspiciously at his friend, who said at last,” Let’s go home.”

A pointy speck of light shone behind the window curtains, as Jim stood before his house at 6 in the morning. He had his arm tightly wrapped around the arm of his friend, who stared dreamily at his home.” It looks quiet.”

“It is. Come on, your brother must be waiting for you.”

“He knows,” Jim asks while looking at Jerry, who replies with a smile. Releasing his arm from the child’s hold, he turns back and begins to leave. Jim turns back towards the deserted alley, seeing his friend leave. Something in him throbs unknowingly at this, but he could only suppress it. He rushes into the house by jumping over the fence and going inside through the courtyard window. His brother Tommy was lying on his bed, reading the cover of the Airman journal. On seeing him, Jim gets anything but startled.

He looks at him defenselessly, waiting for his brother to start the exchange." How did it go with your friend?" he finally coincided with Jim's predictions

"Does Mom know?" Jim questions.

"She believes you're having a sleepover."

Jim scoffs at this and goes towards the bed to lie down beside Tommy." It ends here, isn't it?" Tommy asks

"You sound awful when serious," Jim tells him absurdly and he chuckles at this. Together they stare at the Airman Journal for a time, before noticing writing on the blank side of a picture. Something about the "amends" thing that Jerry had told him then flashes through his mind. He remembers it and didn't cry for some reason.

"It was like this when Dad left," Tommy remarks at last.

He closes the journal, gets up, and rolls over to face his brother's solemn face.

"Jimmy, sometimes it's better to be in the dark." Jimmy stares at his brother, for it is the only thing he was capable of. Instinctively, he held the yellow pouch given to him by his long-gone friend tightly for dear life. The dirty-yellow pouch which had somehow found its way into their conversation became the insignia of their last meetup. Perhaps more so as the tears of the boy streamed out as smoothly as a breeze and as quietly as one can imagine. Another pillow felt the angst in the boy's grip as he clutched onto it like the last resort, bringing it nearer, before burying his face into it. The boy beside him saw the shaken state of his brother but on that day could not bring himself to do anything. At least not for a little while. Until Tommy felt like he was living the moment again .The same moment when he had bawled his eyes out for his lost father. Jim felt the securing of an arm around his shoulders like a snake and looked up from his tears into the tears of his brother.

"Perhaps....it is better to have support, ," and together both fallen ones poured their heart out in an embrace.

A Chance Case

I became a detective that day but not in a way that you think. Sure, I was halfway through my training, initiated by my senior, Mr. Golden Jones, with ten solved cases under his belt . With the rickety reputation of the town police back then, it was pretty bold to have ten cases solved in your name at the police registry. So, overall, it wasn't a bad decision to have him as my model when I started on my training. During these, I benefited greatly from his views on certain cases that appear to be contradicting the normal flow of sense and motive. He told me about the psychological side of cases which remain unique due to their motives and modus operandi. This is where the psychology of the culprit comes into place, but unlike any other reason that directs a crime, it's totally random and often senseless enough to be brushed aside. But I had the due grace of solving one such case while being a trainee only because the main inspector was sick and I had been going across the area of the crime. The circumstances which led me to take hold of the case were as absurd as the case itself. It was pretty simple though. So much so, that its simplicity was the main reason for its being complex. I would have the first impression of being the most unsuitable guy for doing profound research on a case. Let alone reach lengthy conclusions. But something there was in me that somehow benefitted the case. Something which Mr. Jones termed as 'the invaluable advantage', my gut feeling .And that worked well for me.

It started on a sunny morning when I rode my bike across the town square in search of better fuel for the motor. I had been told that there was a mechanic selling crude oil near the old avenue. Having the creasy fame of an amateur detective, it was difficult for me to miss any case taking place in the vicinity. It got through the air of gossip and speculations and into the ears of Mr. Gene Genson, the proud owner of the Genson Grocers. Mr. Genson, with his wrinkly old whiskers and greyish temples, had a knack for favouring one with useful information. It might have happened that when I bought a tad bit more of the flour and oil than required, he exclaimed, “Regur Patt, this might help you in your physique. Let me give you something more for your brain.”

“What is it, Mr. Genson?” I interfered politely.

“There’s info of a burning house, down in Wencrow, catching the ear of the famous detective Josephs. You might have heard of him.”

“The person, yes.”

“Some bigshot among detectives. You might get some brainers from the case. I hear it’s a clingy one.”

“I’ll think about it... Have a good day.” I said, before going over to my bike across the road. The burning house in Wencrow had spread its flames down the whole city, just metaphorically, for when I bent over the fence to look at it, there was just a grimy heap of the building over its greenery, surrounded by the town police of Wencrow with the city police as well as several people in informal clothing, who seemed to be familiar with the situation beforehand, probably detectives. One of the men was a brown-haired shabbily-dressed fellow, who seemed to be juggling through the place, but not in search of a clue. As it turned out, he was the bigshot Josephs I have been listening about. Presently, he sat on an upturned packing case and dug his head into his palms, dejected and drowsy. Before I could take any toll on the situation, a cop showed up at the side instructing me to not eavesdrop, as they had enough with the locals,

"You'll have your share of the matter from the newspaper. I had enough of you people today," he gruffly reminded me.

"I'm Detective Patts of the Vinele Police, next town. I came to hear of the case."

"You know anyone inside?"

"Andrews may know? Anyway, I may be able to help. Your detective there seems depressed," I suggested .

The officer turned his back on me and looked towards the direction in which a lonely figure of a person stooped over a cardboard case. "Yeah, he's a handful. Doesn't work without an assistant."

"I can give some opinion if he may." "Are you a trainee from Vinele?"

"For now, yes."

"Here to fill in for that sick inspector?"

"Not really, but I'm happy to help," I offered eagerly. .

"For your own good, if you can distract him from that bad headache of his, he'd be glad to include you."

"Let's try," I said excitedly and followed the inspector into the property of the owner who perished in the fire . From the first impression, I could only deduce that it was a retired gentleman that owned it evidently due to the location of the house with the accompanying quarters of the servants, presumably all empty. I was acquainted with the experienced detective suffering from a nasty cold, which he argued to have contracted from the weather on the outskirts" It's a bad one altogether. Burning house, sick assistant, sick inspector, and the wary weather-so many tolls for one," he bemoaned upon our arrival.

"Why, Mr. Josephs, I'd be happy to take some of that." I said to lighten the grim atmosphere.

"You should, officer.......... I can't work....under pressure. Have you come in place of that inspector?" Josephs remarked with a hoarse voice "Presumably,"

"Ok, then we must begin. Your company will inform you of the matter at hand. Although, frankly, there's nothing much to explain."

I was visibly irked with that piece of information, for I did so expect something from that chalky black heap of ash and brick bits, yet I persevered to hide my disappointment and looked hopefully towards the officer, for information.

He began, as such, "The house is of a retired Mr. Lawrence Baggs, a property consultant. He had bought it three years ago. It was burned down last night from gasoline. He was on a business meeting with Crayton."

"Does he live alone?" "Yes, a bachelor, to say the least." "Any casualties?"

"None reported. He was off on a deal; servants took a day off. The house was practically empty."

"Anyone know about his departure?" "Servants?"

"They may tell others, who may take advantage of the situation."

The officer replied cockily," For what? Stealing and then burning it to ashes."

"Probably, how was it done?"

"Gasoline, bike fuel. Spread around the exit......."

"....and set ablaze with no one to witness. Was there a canister to pour it?"

"None found here."

I took a moment of my concentration to look at the remains of the old estate. The blackened grass around smelled of wood and ash-coloured smoke billowed from the other devices which had been separated from the debris. Wooden frames and solid cement peeled of their colour lay sprinkled all over the property. Somewhere below the floorboards, sacks of eatables and flour smelled of being overcooked, perhaps if the fire reached the food, it must have reached the parlour and the balcony, scaling every aisle and corner. But no casualties were reported? What for then was the damage done? My mind wandered in the web of these doubts, trying to theorise the motive, identify clues, and catch the culprit, all at that instant. But then I remembered what my instructor had said," All but thinking needs a moment to come to life."

My mind stopped racing and I turned towards my officer, “Who filed the complaint?” I queried brusquely. “Mr. Baggs, himself, through his friend, Mr. Chisels.” “Where’s he? Baggs.”

“In Crayton.” “And his friend?”

“There....” said the officer before pointing towards the main gate around which was spread a police tape, and beyond which stood clumsily, a masked gentleman in overcoat and trousers. He eyed us and waved, confirming his presence. Before I could talk to him, Detective Josephs arrived with ruffled feathers and a flustered expression, “Patts! Do me a favour.” “What is it, sir?”

“Get me a hot coffee from Clayford's, down the street.” “Well, Mr. Josephs, I was hoping to get some intel from Mr. Chisels there.”

“Don’t waste your time. I’ve already done so. And I did get what I wanted.” “Pray let me know. I may learn something.”

“After you get the coffee. This headache is splitting me open .”

I stood there helplessly trying to get the information out of Joseph's but to no avail. The officer standing next to me advised better that I get the coffee. Coming back from Clayford’s, I passed by the main rendezvous of the Wencrow folks. A large bronze statue of a rider partitioned from the greenery around in the garden named, “Abode” It was still filled with people and tourists, children and maidens swinging around the place, all with cheer and chatter. It was followed by a flour grinder. Something had me stop there to satisfy a query that bugged me till then.

“Excuse me, where can I get a bottle of gasoline?” I calmly enquired with a middle-aged man in the shop.

“Right from here, there is a shop called 'Bike Repairs.” he replied. “Is there any other shop? Something nearer to the main road.”

“No, there’s none,” the man responded harshly. There was almost a certain asperity in his voice which compelled me to take a note regarding this fact-” it may be false,”-and I rode off quickly towards the burned-down estate.

“That man, Jeffrey Chisels, knows a great deal about our complainant. It was for him that he moved down to the estates around Boxson's Avenue.” said the detective while gulping down the hot coffee down his throat,” that place stores a great many abandoned complexes here in Wencrow. Ones left desolated by the Perusian princes.”

“Where did you get that from?” I asked in curiosity.

“From the old man himself. He jabbered a great deal about Baggs’ profession concerning the Avenue.”

“As a property consultant, isn’t it?”

“Of course, and he did lend himself an opportunity to sell those run-down properties. Except-”

“Except what?”

The detective downed a spoonful of the sugary concoction and said, "Except he wasn't aware of the danger lurking around the corner .”

“What danger? To his life, you say?”

“Probably? He did make wholesome profits by talking the shareholders into the deal of renting those estates.”

“So, someone was at a loss with his decision?”

“So, they burned down his estate to warn him of the danger.” explained with the last slurp of coffee, a confident air about him. “And how are we to find the culprit?” I asked.

“A sneaky one? Think about it later.” said the Detective. “What now, then?”

“Talk to the neighbours and servants. Get a reality check. Then, we'll be better able to assess the situation.”

As directed and theorised by the detective, I went on with the regular questioning of the people nearby and those involved in the life of Mr. Baggs, who for one had not yet shown his face. To summarise, here was a man whose house had been burned down to ashes in response to some deed that he had done and who was now unavailable yet soulful enough to send the police after the culprit. To me, it was the general antics of grey-haired folks but it was not the whole of me that believed it. While drowsing myself in these distractions, I met several characters across the property, who were close acquaintances of Mr. Baggs but did not live in the vicinity. And the surprising factor of it was that none of them was local. It was this fact that reminded me further of the absence of some piece in this mystery. One Mr. Sanders of Greenville met me with the same amazement-cum-subtlety that I had seen upon the face of Chisels. As I reached nearer, the man grew older and a flicker of subtle shock was visible on his brows.

"Mr. Sanders, do you live here?"

"Not currently. But I occasionally rent the Amerd's Villa in Boxson's Avenue."

"For what purpose may I know?"

"For the glamour and entertainment. It is a fine place to dine and meet friends."

"What profession?",

"Well, I've dabbled in the stock market and banking over the years."

"So, a banker, you say."

"Yes, but retired although I do get a pension." "How long have you known him?"

"About a year and a half. He aided me in renting the Amerd's." "Ok, Mr. Sanders, have you by any chance known people who would despise Mr. Baggs?"

"Well, it seems unlikely. But I am not that efficiently acquainted with Baggs' life before Wencrow, except that he consulted the bigshots regarding properties."

"Do you know from whom can I get that information?"

"Well, his closest one is Mr. Chisels, I don't know him myself. But their relations date back to college times." said Sanders, whose suggestive tone compelled me to eye across the area in search of Chisels, but he was nowhere to be found.

"Perhaps he has gone back," I mused, which was loud enough for Sanders to inform me of his abode," He lives at that emerald-crossed villa at the avenue."

"How far is it from here?"

"About twenty," guessed Sanders.

The tone of the day was shifting to turn gloomier, with the shrinking of the sun rays, and as I bid farewell to my restless superior, who had been on and off about the registry at Crayton to talk to people there about our complainant, an itchy desire rang through me. Gazing out at the deserted street, the silence was profound and intimidating enough to send my thoughts into a spiral of doubts and questions.it was half past ten at most. You'd say it's absent-mindedness but as the thought of what I was longing for hit me, my hands grabbed the handle of my bike and fueled the ignition, and I sped off into the lonely streets of Wencrow, in search of the nearest gas shop.

My search came to fruition when at last I came upon the closest I could find, a dingy one at that, monitored by a youth in shorts and a journal. I went up to him, and after giving him a compensation for my untimely questioning, secured the information-of the type of canister he used for storing the gasoline. Fun fact: it was a red-shaded one. Going speedily about the road, I could only think of the next day to begin my search. If I were to go into the details of my questioning and the purpose of it, it would solely be in regard to the case, except that it also concerns the people absent throughout the day.

The next day was another sunny adventure for the likes of me, along with my irritative superior, who had skillfully questioned the servants of the estate about the incident, while I listened to it intently, clinging to the hope of catching an irk here and a worry there on the servants' face. There was Ricardo, a man-servant from overseas whom Baggs had taken in while being off-shore on a meeting with his former employer. Then, there was a seamstress, Angela, sharp and quick-witted who had met her employer while being a nanny at the south parlour area. There were a few who had been employed from the nearer towns, Vilene one of them, but other than that, their characteristics seemed pretty bland to my superior.

To me, they seemed pretty loyal and truthful, so much so that I had the urge to satisfy my curiosity with them about one question. Ricardo seemed the perfect one for that. A bulky man in his thirties, he was the personification of the word 'valour' and to add to it, he had a stupefying mustache. As Josephs sprung away from the quarters and into the glimmering day ahead, I went up to the servant and urged his assistance in answering my doubts. He dutifully obliged and while going across the property, I asked, "Was your master really under a threat?"

"Sir, I already answered that to the mister there. He looked tense after that letter he was sent."

"And the letter was sent from?"

"It wasn't from the postal. Someone just slipped it through the slit in the door."

"Was he a local?"

"Not sure. I didn't see anybody outside. Maybe the letter had been left like that much before."

"When the house was off guard." "Probably, when no one was around-" "Or sleeping,"

"Did Mr. Baggs hold any meetings at the house regarding his work?" "Sometimes his friends or clients come to visit. It was mostly casual, though."

"One more thing, Ricardo, did Baggs engage in a brawl with any of the locals?"

"Well, I wouldn't be sure of that, but a man did cause a difference here once," "Who was it?"

"He only spoke to Mr. Baggs." "And you heard?"

"Not really, although it did escalate towards the end,"

"Any details about him?" I asked hopefully but got the answer in negative.

"Ok," It was assured by the third day of this case and by the second day of knowing him that John Josephs, the bigshot was at a crossroads with me. While the theory formed by him about the warning and all aligned perfectly with sense, it missed some loose ends. It was initially hard then to go against the big game when you're a newbie yourself. I made up my mind about meeting Mr. Chisels that day at Boxson's to talk to him in person about the case, and as the party of investigators settled in for the day at noon, I rode off to Boxson's, which stood impressively among the oak and the agriculture, near Wencrow. For clarity, it stood somewhere in the border between Wencrow and the jungle of the font, bearing an impressive collection of fine estates as tall as the mahogany itself, one of which belonged to Jeffrey Chisels, a broker by profession and gambler by choice. This house which he so proudly owned near the other estates had been the product of one such game, which his friend had saved him from. Paying not distraction to this fact, I rang the doorbell of the door, bearing an emerald on the crafted wood. The old broker opened it and was rather pleased to see me, maybe in hopes of getting an update about the case. He gladly ushered me to the spacious living room of the house, where having placed myself comfortably on one of the sofa seats, I began,

"Well, Mr. Chisels, as you know of the matter, I would not dwell into the details, except that there's no update about it."

"Then, why have you alighted as such?" the old man replied hoarsely," I have told everything to the detective,"

"Yes, but I have some questions about it," I answered. "Pray to tell."

"Who informed you of the house burning?"

"A local, I'd say. He got my number from one of the servants who had gone out for the day."

"What did he say?"

"That that the house had burned down," "And nothing else,"

"Not in particular,"

"Did you tell Baggs about this exchange when you contacted him?" "Maybe, I was too traumatized with the news already,"

"And then?"

"Then he told me to contact the police about it,"

"Isn't it strange for him to not be present here, now? What can you say about it?"

"Well, it may be that he is traumatised by the incident, his fears had come to the surface with this one,"

"What fears? He did know of the danger, right?" "He was certain something like this would happen." "So why did he not say it?"

The old man was unsure of it, and he showed this with a tiresome expression.

"How about the town?" "Wencrow?"

"Why did he come here in the first place?"

"Wanted to settle in some near countryside like this, not to retire but live up to his promises,"

"And by promises, you mean?" "Commitments to his wife, Linda."

"So that was the sole reason? And the dealings he did here was to follow it?"

"He is a man of actions, does what he needs and wants to do, sometimes brimming others in the process. You wouldn't have been coming here if it weren't for his complaint,"

"And the fact that it was a warning," I claimed and was met with a knowing gaze," then, why isn't he coming here?"

"Owns his antics,"

The broker's calmness flustered me . I realised then that I had come unprepared in front of him, regarding the doubts and queries. It somehow got lost in my mind while pondering upon the possible conclusions. The servants dispersed, the house possibly destroyed and a sense of foreboding that compelled him to restrict his visit, all raced my mind in the instant that we were quiet. Having no probable questions to satisfy, I went my way out of the house, gladly escorted by the owner himself who had the grace of introducing me to the property. And was it worth trudging for? This and other fairly larger establishments were surrounded by eclectic acres of trees and blossoms, each giving way to newness and extravagance, and possible income if exploited. Here was a tree, a humongous crown of leaves , impressive of his girth and expressive of his majesty, as it covered the entire of an area of Tussocky grass in its embracing shade. Another lay curled up in the shade of its bigger fellow, with coloured leaves and a curly spine. The flowers, white and yellow, swayed in the movement of the evening breeze in perfectly smooth mud and neatly tilled soil.

"A genuine beauty, it is," said Chisels dreamily. "One of the reasons for the value,"

"What type?" I enquired about the vegetation.

"The flowers you see are grown and handled while the grass breeds just about anywhere."

"And the trees?"

"Well, it is its creation," said the old man.

It inspired me with a sudden burst of energy to look at the 'genuine beauty' and admire its position in the outskirts, for where it had been a tad bit nearer to the town, it would have possibly taken a share..

'A tad bit.......' I mused, "How was it before you came here?"

"Here? Pretty much the same, except a few of the trees being cut down to provide way for the gravel path" and with the beckoning of his fingers, he showed me the gravel path, sliding beautifully from among a bunch of stems.

Another trip from a possible tip-off and something was at hand. The man, the promise, the obstinacy, and the brawl. One piece had come to place-that of the stubbornness of Baggs to come here, which although unclear made for a character sketch of our person. 'Man, of action', fiery and possibly ambitious, so much so that he did not heed anyone, someone's warning and thus, the result. But it must be possible, I thought, that by his absence, he was trying to provoke the culprit, to urge him to make some mistake............... or so maybe to scare him. If it was to provoke, it might have been that the person is of some depth and ferocity; otherwise, if it was to scare him, the list of suspects somehow shortens and shrinks, about the size incorporating a small town as Wencrow.

On seeing a small store on my way bearing a telephone exchange, I quickly acted on my instincts and went on to ask the owner about the list of people in the past few days who had spared a call or two, here, of

course, after compensating him for the same. Having, thus, earned his good grace, I also enquired about the appearance of such people who appeared unusual, giving the necessary character tropes.

It was sundown by the time I reached the burned manor, seeing a policeman roaming and chatting about as usual. I found my officer and asked him about the whereabouts of my superior,

"His headache took the better of him, although he had some clues before going," the officer replied.

"Pray to tell," I asked with no more thrill and excitement as I had foretold already that this was to go at a crossroads with my theory.

The following night, as I scrutinized the lawn after dark, a thin figure near the fence caught my eye. His clothes suggested a local. He was bending, trying to squeeze through a gap. On a dutiful interference of mine from a few yards away, he abruptly looked haywire and began to bustle about like some drunkard. Probably not knowing the way with legal binding, he suspiciously took a curve along the half-lit road and disappeared into the darkness. As I took my turn into the road, beginning to dive into the same train of thoughts, the headlight of my bike flashed on the lone figure of the same man. I noticed his dark-brown eyes pointed straight at me, and there was a sort of steadfastness and brevity in that stare, so much so that I almost got distracted by it and was about to hit a tree, a while ahead. This slowed my stead and forced me to stop the bike for the time being. The lone figure of the fellow which still gazed at me with his death stare, was about half a kilometre in the front. Suddenly, he began to charge towards me with a certain speed. All regarding the culprit and the manor flashed before me in fury. Perhaps I had missed a lead and the culprit is just a rash fellow, bearing a primitive grudge. Whatever it was or had been, came racing up at that moment. I instinctively took my hand on the back of my waist, over the revolver, and shouted,

"Who are you!"

"Are you a detective?" another voice came in reply with no sign of anxiety at earshot.

"Yes, who are you?" I repeated.

"I'm a friend," the man replied savagely after halting in front of me. The sense of comfortability in his manner which culminated in a slight grin from his lip edges rang through me,

"Are you going over that case?" he said while pointing with his index finger towards the burned mansion.

"What interests you?" I said coldly.

"Calm down, officer. I am a confidant of Mr. Baggs." With this, he began to take out an envelope from the back pocket of his pants. Placing it in between his thumb and index finger, he said, "He has this for you,"

"How would I know so?" I asked

"He was previously on a business venture in Crayton, a real-estate venture, to levy some recognition to the puritan-architectural estates on the outskirts." he began. "I was acquainted with him while he was moving to Wencrow and have aided him in his work since then "

I loosened my grip over the sack and was about to take the envelope when the man hid it behind him, "Not here,"

His cautious resistance urged me to change the setting of our meetup elsewhere. After a quick trip back to Vilene and stopping near an old bar, invited him in and bided him to continue the story. As we sat beyond the bar, this young man began again,

“He had been restless ever since news of the incident came, who wouldn’t be? But in his behaviour, it was apparent that he had been expecting something of this kind, let alone getting surprised by it. You know what he was restless about?”

“What?!” I asked meekly.

“Something that was to occur but hadn’t yet. That was why in this aggravation, he had at first instant, called for the police, to execute his reply.”

“What about the letter?”

The lad hadn’t forgotten about it, so he searched into his waist pocket looking at me apologetically and brought out the red-coloured envelope in front of me. On it were the initials, ‘L.B.’, printed in gold. I opened it and took out the white piece of paper wrapped neatly. It read:

The whole selected paragraph is distorted. This can be the possible paragraph:

I apologize for having you see this dark topic that requires my presence, but I am no less eager to reveal the mystery that you are here to solve. Alas! Some awkward circumstances have prevented me, but I will try to put the situation in front of you as unbiasedly as I can.

The matter might be related to the entire town of Wencrow, a happy little constituency with flourishing trade and youth. But the heart of certain people there has instilled a particular sense of patriotism towards the ruins of their hinterland. Some of the ancestors of this town for centuries tried their agriculture and green spaces beyond the threshold of their own province, evidently seeking a lush and vibrant atmosphere for the Puritans to settle for some time, in present-day Boxson Avenue.

Let's just say, the building of population in the old estates has rather infuriated some locals, one of whom was bold enough to straight away complain to me about it. He was concerned that the hedge would be rooted out, the trees cut, and the grass rolled up for grazing. But the most important to him were the sweet blossoms that harbored the pollinators - the sweet daisies, the cheerful daffodils, and the daring sunflowers. All that has been bred and perfected by his relatives - their very existence being under threat, he was sure of.

I have comforted him with the thought that it would be protected, but the spirit of youth in the most unexpected aspect of this situation. I do hope to be providing some clues to you about the matter, and request you to prevent such things from happening again, if it is planned to. Frankly, I do sense a mishap in the making. Yours thankfully,

Lawrence Baggs.

I was certain of some facts that the story presented, but the whole picture still seemed unclear, for it somehow felt as though Mr. Baggs was underpinning some of the valuable hints.

'A man of action', I had recalled his friend saying about him, and yet in the tone with which he had narrated the events, seemed overwhelming and sensitive.

"He wrote this?" I asked the man in front of me, who was surprised by this inquiry.

"Why, you would have been sure of it, had you noticed his penmanship," the man replied.

"Well, I haven't,"

"It must've been in a hurry,"

I decided to accept his reasoning but in some way, the mystery of that man hovering over our complainant and finally burning down his house for some reason seemed far-fetched–How anyone could be so agitated enough to burn down someone's manor after initially meeting him two or three times?

"Well, did Mr. Baggs ever talk about this person?" I enquired after a brief pause.

"Oh, the boy. Sometimes he talks a lot." "What does he say?"

"About the boy's clothes, his demeanour, smile," "After only meeting him two or three times?"

"I'm not sure of that fact, but I guess they had a good number of conversations before he went to Crayton for the trip?"

"Is he in Crayton now?"

"Probably," the man replied unsure of what he said as he was for the time skimming through a bag of postcards and letters,

"Here.... this one's dated to a few years back before I met him,"

I took the old wrinkled envelope, braided with the same initials, L.B., and expectantly read the letter, which went:

The whole selected paragraph is distorted. This can be the possible paragraph:

It is with a sense of guilt and regret that I write this letter, obviously not owed to you, but due to the circumstances in which I find myself. Mr. Bob has finished nearly a year in Prague, where he decided to take off from there to some unknown destination that he wouldn't tell me about, and I have been worried sick ever since. Linda is also not keeping well.

Unfortunately, for the very same reasons, I would be unable to meet you at 7:00 o'clock this evening, and I may have to take some days off from the project. Nevertheless, I will make sure to keep the will of this project at hand, for whenever Mr. Grip decides to play strong. Until then, I bid you farewell and offer my congratulations.Yours thankfully,

Lawrence Baggs.

“He had a boy?” I asked after folding the letter.

“Oh, yes, a long time ago. But he disappeared some years ago, or better yet living in some cold continent,” the man replied, “Well, Mr. Detective, I have given you the information which Mr. Baggs had wished to inform you about,”

“Did he also instruct you to return as soon as possible?”

“No, he’s cool. He told me to take a few days off to watch over the savannah in the east,” he said, “It was nice meeting you, though,”

With this, he stood up and began taking pace towards the doorway. From the day that I took this case, I felt the uncertainty of facts for the whole situation and how it restricts the owner from setting foot on his property. It seemed vague and stupid for someone to do so and yet the spirit of youth.................

"Hey!" I shouted at the top of my voice towards the doorway, from where my acquaintance was just about to cross the threshold when He looked back at me, startled , "What's your name?"

"Oh, I'm Theo Mades" "Theo, how did you get here?" "By car"

"Does Mr. Baggs own a car?"

"Oh, he had given me his car for the occasion," "Where is it?"

"In Wencrow."

"Would you be able to accompany me to Wencrow now?" I requested after a pause.

"Sure, Officer."

Together, we retraced our steps back to Wencrow, and it wasn't wholly for the purpose of examining Mr. Baggs' car. On the way, I stopped for a refill at the gas station and asked the owner a suitable question, to which he gladly streamed his expertise onto the matter. "Well, from the bigger cities, you take a walk to the station and catch the bus nearest to the front up ahead. And you get down at the signpost two acres back from the outskirts. From there, walk your way up the gas station." the owner narrated.

"That's the cheapest way?" "Of course."

Resuming the journey, we got past the beautiful garden and the burned mansion, at which point, my companion began to inquire about our destination, to which I replied, “It isn’t too far,”

And it was not, for when we reached Boxson’s Avenue, the light from several of the street lamps illuminated the streets and houses, many of them empty but taken care of. Parking my bike a foot from the glow and into the shadows, I asked my companion, “You know of Mr. Chisels?”

“Yes, does he live here?” he asked and I replied with a nod.

There in the calm and freezing shadows of the tall trees, the one with the massive shade, I talked my companion into standing beside it. From where we could see the park gate to the plot clearly.

“Why, are we waiting for someone?” “Yes, for now. What’s the time?”

“Ten–thirty,” he replied while glancing at his watch. “It shouldn’t be more than half an hour,”

“Half an hour, we have to stand here,”

“It’ll pass,”

It did pass after the gentle breeze turned its gaze upon the greenish-yellow leaves and the grass beneath it, which rustled furiously and gave the faint smell of a hundred new fruits. The blossoms for the season too glided unobtrusively in the night, giving out the fresh aroma of a thousand springs in advance. And while the tree stumps stood perfectly agile and maintained its shade, the wind went gleeful and forceful by the minute, such that by the thirtieth of it, the leaves above us rustled violently along with their counterparts. But the wait was over for that, as sometime after the thirtieth minute, the street lamps shut out all light and the alley turned as dark as the shade, the sky as bright as the glow from the moon. "Oh, has the power gone out?"

"No, the lights give out at 11," "So, our wait is over."

"Presumably, our wait is now numbered."

Even in the seeming darkness, the faint lighting of the estates gave out some visibility and the most prominent of it was the mansion of the emerald stone,

"It's glowing," I confirmed, "Is that where he lives?"

"Yes, and we have to watch out for someone coming from the park gate." The gate was admittedly visible enough to make out the presence of any individual crossing it. While the extreme lumens of the headlight at the desired house would make for the person's presence as such. I had a certain gut exclaiming me to watch out and be careful, to count the minutes until the presence alighted at the set doorsteps. And it did after fifteen minutes of silence, a figure smoothly coming from the nearest street and crossing the park gate, casually, although it did not take me a second to get alerted and instruct my companion to do the same. The figure stopped after the gate, seeming to scan his surroundings for any possible trap, only getting the whooshes of the blowing wind in return. It calmly, advanced towards the plot, passing several of the bigger estates, before halting before the door of the emerald gem, encrusted on its chest. The figure knocked on the door and was later admitted by a person behind the door, who peeked from the slight opening of the door. The identity was satisfied and the figure of a man went into the house.

"Do we have to wait for more?"

"Count to five minutes," I said assuredly, "Then, we'll go in,"

The three-hundredth second passed, and we swept down the grass toward the emerald-encrusted door.. Once near, I put my ear to the door but was greeted with silence. Seeming to take a toll on my companion's patience, I gently knocked at the door. A few minutes later came the sound of feet walking on the wooden floor, whose intensity increased by a second.

"Who is it?" a voice came from inside.

"Mr. Chisels, will you open up?" I asked in a professional, but meek, tone. "Detective?" the voice replied, "Are you here for something"

"Yes, I wanted to ask you about something. Will you please open the door?"

After a pause, a rail was lifted and the door slid back a little to reveal the puffy countenance of Mr. Jeffrey Chisels,

"What do you want, Detective?"

"Calm down, Mr. Chisels, please open the door?"

"What business do you have at this hour? I demand—" Before he could finish his plea, I slammed the door open and rushed inside to the living room just before Mr. Chisels could react. Inside perched on the sofa where two individuals whom I had never seen before, were seated, one with a solemn demeanour and the other quite casual as before. "Mr. Baggs?" my companion replied while eyeing the older individual, "What are you doing here?"

Seeing us, the younger one froze, shock quickly turning into contempt for the man seated beside him.

“What is all this? You tricked me.” the youth shouted and pointed towards the older one, evidently Mr. Baggs.

“No, it isn’t as such, Mathias. Just sit for a while. "Mr. Baggs replied after securing his composure.

Before the youth could show his spirit, I said, “Well, Mr. Baggs, the present circumstances which you had written about hadn’t quite matched my theory, so I headed out to dig. Of course, if you were to return to Wencrow without coming in the radar, you would definitely take the least viable route,”

“Well, officer, it isn’t the way you presume,”

“I know that, Mr. Baggs. That is why I am here. If you can make a clean breast of things now, it’ll all go smoothly for you.........” I exclaimed, pointing toward the younger individual, “and for him, which you regard

as your son,”

The man began to regain his ability of recollection, sewing the circumstances and events that led to this day, and then began dutifully, “Well, before I moved to Wencrow, I lived peacefully on the west coast of the district of Andison. I decided to move here after she died of Cholera three years ago,”

“Here, you met him, didn't it?” I interfered

“Yes, he had a knack for numbers, so I hired him for the same. It so happened that at a certain point in time, the estates here at Boxson’s caught my attention, possibly abandoned and ancient enough to be in high price. I had a word with some of the prominent people in the field of my profession. Having to let them know of this was accomplishing."

"But it didn't cede well with the locals,"

"Admittedly, they feared that if tourists began to reside in these houses, it would affect their control over the forest outside,"

"That it would get ruined, and what's with this fellow?"

The old man began to prepare himself to face the young man who stood beside him, and he pleadingly looked at him,

"He isn't at fault. The hooligans back there provoked him to do what he did,"

My eyes rolled back to the stout figure standing beside me. From his eyes, poured a mixture of rage and desperation in quick blinks,

"Did you burn down the house?" I questioned him authoritatively. "Yes, I did," he replied skillfully

"How did you do so? With the red canister full of kerosene,"

The lad looked puzzled but finally said, "Yes".

I chuckled from inside and gazed at him with some more inquiries, "Well, why did you burn the mansion? Did you want your employer gone thinking that if he goes away from Wencrow, no houses will be monetised and people will come? Isn't that what you thought?"

"Yes, I did. So that Mr. Baggs won't be buzzing over here," "Well, then why are we here? Mr. Baggs?"

The old man looked up from the floor and into my eyes, with despondence and hopelessness in his every word, "I came in for a settlement with him in return for taking the case back,"

"And what's the point in sending me the letter?" "I did want you catch the culprit, the real one," "So, Mr. Baggs, you think, Mathias is innocent."

He is protecting his townsfolk," the old man said hoarsely, "All of them who want the blossoms fresh and the wind rustling over the leaves,"

The matter was nearing resolution, but the identity of the real culprit remained vague and uncertain for the one thing which was needed to call it even was the fact that if the young man did swear to the identity of the culprit, he would be released from suspicion. Yet it wasn't what our complainant wanted. More than catching the culprit, he wanted the young man to be declared innocent. I had so for the same. "Mr. Mathias. You may have to give a full account of the case and your part in it. But not here." I adjourned the following night with this.

The next morning, we found us near the Vilene Police Station, where the suspect under charge was being interrogated about the possible ways in which the incident took place. During this, he was supposed to write an account of the incident on a blank sheet of paper. Waving that account in his hand, the burly officer of the town police came to me,

"This will be enough for a charge, Patts," he said.

"Well, before submitting it, will you please check for the handwriting in the threat given to Mr. Baggs?

Have an expert come by, if necessary," I replied, "You know, just for the record"

But the writing was not a match in this case, implying that a second culprit was at large regarding such. The young man was further coaxed by the police then, to give up his name. But I had gotten him in this pickle, in a way to challenge his obstinacy. The police wouldn't rest until they got the name of his accomplice. Further investigations will be undergone and he will be charged extensively for nothing., I had known that from studying the psychological side of the culprit that the motive and reason didn't always come into play. It was the mental side that I had to focus on to catch the conspirators.

That a man may favour his companions but not to the point where he may suffer for nothing, "Ah, the spirit of youth is senseless, for some" I mused while going over the case a while later.

It became known that after much coaxing, Mathias Shelton had finally broken up with his patience. As it were, being born into a complacent neighbourhood, favouring one another and raised occasionally by a neighbour, he might have come into someone whom he owed a good deed. That is why, when he got wind of a burning near the Hills, he rushed there to find his employer's house in flames, with a bunch of people around it. They occasionally despised the fellow for ruining their ancestors' legacy, for money. He had earlier complied with them and worked as a mediator in their arguments. But to this extent it would reach, he wasn't sure of. Evidently, the people had molded him into favoring them for something or the other, for old times' sake.. As it turned out, you really have to take a look at the mannerisms of certain individuals to catch the conspiracy behind their masks and the fact is more prominent in younger ones.

As for Mr. Baggs, he might have been flooded with the nostalgia of the familiarity that the youth shared with his son, his long-lost heir. At a point where he is alone and lonely, when he sees him standing all ambitious and free-spirited, it reminds him of warmth and hope. Although I didn't deduce at first, my mentor Mr. Jones, when I met him two days after Shelton was taken in custody.

With a solemn expression and casual demeanor, he bent over the chair with coffee in his hands and said,

"A man, no matter where he goes, cannot escape his past; it's better to overcome it."

"How is that relevant, sir?"

"Relevant is the fact that there are many youthful spirits in this world who may bear a certain likeness to another in their youthfulness. Shelton had one with the boy that took off from Prague and never returned."

He had his usual ritual of grinning before sipping.

"So, nothing serious about this affair," I asked. "None so far. There are no deaths, of course.

Only that the ugliest of man's emotions had worked its way out.

Charm of the blue pearl

One quiet October night, I found myself scaling the nearly empty, half-lit streets of the town of Bleakstone, out of mere whim and boredom. The glow from the old-rusty street lights fell upon the asphalt roads, leaving the footpath to doll in the darkness. Except for the few homes bearing the presence of night owls and insomniacs–considering it was close to bedtime–the town had gone into a considerable slumber. Above were the brilliant arrays of stars sprinkled around the sky such that it did seem to try its best to light up this less-frequented and more-explored part of the town.

From the distance, there was a queue of buildings and shops lined up on either side of the street, most of which were shuttered down or locked shut. The sudden burst of urge found me in that ungodly hour on that ungodly path, surrounded by none other than silence and superstitions was itself unknown and abysmal. Perhaps it stemmed from my insatiable urge for adventure in low-lying caves, treacherous jungles, or most simply in a back alley of a building..........surrounded by dumpsters and shabby-haired cats and grumpy-eyed mongrels. That is what roused me from sleep at eleven, put on my shoes and went warily into the chilly air of the night........... Whatever the invisible urge it was, I was all in for it.

Lights had given and were giving way to the monotonous shrilling of a distant nightling with a speck of anticipation here and there. Houses were bolted into secrecy. The town cuddled and snored. You might as well say that the night was lonely and needed a friend. I was the nominee.

A few dedicated souls, lights glowing in their windows were packing up for the day. All but one, of course.

A sparkling shop sign of a store aloof from the dazzle and company of all others caught my wandering eyes, for it read 'Andre Antics' in a cursive script. Almost at the near end of the complex, it bore the expression of being the abode of nocturnal. A sick, yellowish glow hovered around the shop, doing little to light its grumpier surroundings. As I casually meandered nearer to it, the spookiness of the area seemed to heighten and expand to form a single mass of force, pushing me nearer to the entrance.

A little more of that same energy and I found myself on the threshold of the store, before an eerily-designed door, blood red. A look through the clear glass fitted beside the door and I gazed at the several pieces of art, old jewellery, and door frames stashed on a corner. The display had nothing on it, save for the lights around it, meant to glorify the item on display. I touched the door handle and pushed it, which led to a wooden floor on the inside.

The interior was far more cluttered than its exterior suggested. The several stages of items were a part of the masquerade of antique sitting on glass fitted on the walls of the old store. The walls were yellowed and the plaster was slinging from one place onto the thick wood over the floor. A jumble of items - vases, necklaces, cricket bats, and baseball caps - filled the glass cases, hinting at their potential value and history.

The creamy-coloured lighting came from four light bulbs placed on four sides of the ceiling–one of them was flickering incessantly over a mantelpiece bearing the baseball cap. All of these at once fooled me enough from noticing the small desk situated in the northeast corner of the shop, seating a cross-eyed fellow in a blue cap and clothing in various shades of grey. When I noticed him unconditionally staring at me with those dark-brown pupils pointing at me like the barrels of a pistol, my heart skipped a beat looking at the bulky, huge, hairy, and practically still rendition of a person born to sit still and scared the balls out of an intruder. His eyes seemed to dictate me to extol the purchase. Something in the heart of man compelled me to look towards the glass casings of ancient historical items and not elsewhere. My eyes set in motion searching for a meagerly cheap item for purchase, the choices ranging from the baseball cap, the flower vase, a thick and circular disc, some earrings, and even a flat stone.

Suddenly it came into sight, perching on the top of a stirrup, holding the metal chain of its whole figure such that, one can notice the shimmering and dazzling of its body in full focus and aim—of the blue pearl atop the mantelpiece above the cap. It seemed to be the speck of the blue of the deep sea and the blue of the morning sky at the same time, to be the sparkle of the sunshine and the crawling in the darkness at the same instant. When my hands sped along to hold the pearl-encrusted over by a copper casing, it was a cheery bright blue. Placing it on the counter, I had nearer eye contact with the bulky fellow, who now had an assortment of wrinkles on his forehead. His hands at the counter held the droopy fat above it and suddenly he seemed like seventy, but with the same fury glance at me-the gaze of it seemed to put me in a boiler room or a sauna, as perspiration had settled on my temple, my throat had gulped the last ounce of saliva and my heart was crumpling rather than beating. Instinctively I dug into my pockets, taking out everything I had from last time's exchange and putting it on the counter. Taking the pearl, I made for the door and into the needling fresh wind of the night sky. The air inside was choking. The wind was wild and adventurous and as I had the tingling of my senses, being out from the store, it urged me for another.

I sprinted through the desolate streets between a long array of houses, dark and still, sleepy and ignorant. The wind currents raced with me and went past me, taking out all the sweat and sense of being. When I did stop at a swirl, all but me was left, for I didn't feel my chest heaving and swaying, my feet swelling, my arms cramping and aching, and my nose bludgeoned by the wind to senselessness. Seeing far into the horizon which was blocked by the buildings, one of it glowed vibrantly and stood out from its companions. A creamy yellow light brightened the street after it, the sign of the shop printed on it. As I curiously strained my eyes, the bright glow emanating from the fist had my eyes staring at my open palm on the sparkling light-blue pearl, or as it were the glowing end of a star. It was so fresh and vibrant.

My feet attempted to wander groggily into the darkness, towards the light, by virtue of some mesmerizing force, as a blue pearl burnt with its glow, dangling from a closed fist,.

From my perspective

To describe human nature in a nutshell well, that would be too small. To describe human nature in a shell of the necessary size, that is to provide a summation of my experiences growing among the very beings, as , in the Barrygong Park, it is somewhat unexpected at best and amusing at least.

Nonetheless, I have never failed to witness some of the characteristic instances in the lives of my counterparts–frankly, I do not have anything else to take an interest in. To begin with, A young banyan tree (a mere 50 years old), I stand in the heart of Barrygong Park, a haven for social gatherings, friendly encounters, and lively conversations.

From the moment that I sprouted from the dry surface of my landing, it had been known to me that humans are a whole lot of beings, having the most entertaining of anecdotes and experiences to narrate to, and others to reside in, saving the latter part of entertainment involving hand gestures and profanities to take toll of anyone's conscience for later. I have nevermore been correct when I thought of seeking the bright side of it, in view of the declining grace of the stars at night and the weather being considerably tacky and stubborn.

For, though, there had come a lot of disappointments–as in during the beating of a crowd of protestors, ruining my shade with a bunch of flowers and solemn and tear-stricken faces at sight, killing of my comrades—on the whole, it was and has been an exciting journey with the common sense that these warm-blooded mammals put into their everyday life.

Many of the activities take place in the vicinity with the first rays of the sun falling on the top of my head, when I see joggers circling the park with a sense of accomplishment, although some of them have a sully face, as though they are being forced by some invisible force to take strides and jump here and there. But the better part of my focus remains engraved towards those rare incidents of collisions and disagreements when a lot of voices ring through the air at the same time, accompanied by some shallow settlements of apology between one or the other. One such time when the rays of the sun were rather furious and burned my temples, a commotion erupted somewhere near the cement track, circling the park. There were a lot of people jammed in one spot, moving hands and shouting into the crowd.

At the juncture of this incident, my focus should have been on the centre of that human confusion, to the person creating the ruckus and disorder, if not for a certain swirl of water into the ground with the simultaneous retreat of a bottle on the road. It had been dug to the floor by a hot-headed individual from the confusion, and the owner of that item–a frail young woman–lay motionless as if to signal her annoyance with this unruly behaviour. She was even about to voice her grievance to the person, if not a young man had come into the way between the crowd and the woman, gently lifting the bottle and apologising on behalf of the whole crowd of human confusion.

The young man's charm softened the woman's appeal and presently she complied, even admiring the fellow for his judicious behaviour.

This was enough for my imagination to dwindle in the way as I thought of this exchange a little later into the night when all was quiet and unknown. I had known in my twentieth year of the possible friendship between humans of different genders or sexes, and a different sort of friendship, not the one I had with the rose or the grass or with the sky. It was a mystery to me and I was thrilled to seek for a moment in order to dig deep into this mystery.

My expectations had heightened when this particular exchange provided a difference from my other observations of interactions between men and women–that the girl attempted to talk to the guy a little later by the sprinklers, and he dutifully, or rather graciously, agreed. Thus, began my intensive study of this particular interaction.

From that day, perhaps, I waited for quite a number of first rays to recognize the pair, but to no avail. Yet that exciting day was at hand, when after another starless and dim night, with the first rays falling on the backside of my body, I saw the young man striding across the road. Finally, sitting on the rusty bench (fortunately, just opposite to me), the man began fidgeting on some square-shaped device and went on with it, until he was interrupted by the young lady in tracks. His face took a cheerful expression, and together they held another hour-long conversation, jabbering and gnawing, often showing teeth and smiling, and when the golden rays began covering the grass in a spree, they stood up and walked towards the entrance, together. It had been more than a justifiable expression of emerging friendship, but what was so different?

As this question kept wriggling me, I had a burst of patience erupt into my mind, deciding to wait for the story to unfold. A good memory serves you at last–as I had dutifully memorised the variable freckles on the young woman's cheek and the slight hint of hair growing below the man's nose after the two encounters, it didn't take long to sort out them from the bustling population, which had begun to scatter over the park before dawn.

Once in the evening, I noticed them among a pair of older couples by a snack stand in the park, feeding one another and rarely aiming to enjoy the mouth-watering items (I measured the level of satisfaction in the food when I saw a child gobble up all that was in the plate before the next wind swirled) there was to enjoy. And on another, that time, some rays later, they merrily sat on the grass taking pleasure in the ebbing of the rays and receding of the sun. Judging from the child's enthusiasm in gobbling up the dish, I figured that the taking of one plate would somehow cause a disagreement or two between the pair, except that it was not so. At the end, I figured that the young man might not be the hungry and fastidious soul by which I had known most of my counterparts; he selflessly held the plate whole the woman ate from it. Although I did not understand what he was smiling at the woman for.

As rays went spreading and shrinking, their familiarity with one another increased with the frequency of visits to this place. On the contrary, it practically bored me to a point when I did not notice any difference in their relationship from that of anyone having a friendship with someone of the same gender. Although I do ponder that it did not matter that much as the point of socialising, as I had learned, was to not feel out of place from the world, as humans have a considerably hard time being alone. In this case, I find myself superior to my counterparts as I had lived by imagination and observations up until now and will continue to live so for another eternity to come.

But as to the story, if I say that I know the ending of it, I would be half-right about it, for the interactions between the freckled woman and invisible mustachioed man ended quite abruptly and unknowingly. As it goes that after several of the interactions being in the span of thirty mundane nights, suddenly it so happened that they stopped (or ended as I thought then). There have been no familiar pairs in the park for a long time and it took a toll on my hair. I really do not like such endings where the end is unknown. I wandered along for a long time around the park, near the cement track, on the benches, and around the crowded snack shops, which had increased in frequency, presenting several more of the dainty dishes for the hungry souls. I often came upon other pairs, having similar conversations in similar setups under similar circumstances, all but one that I had been seeking the end to.

On one fateful bright day, my patience was rewarded when I saw the young man with a hint of a mustache, which had begun to intensify below his aquiline nose. He was without a smile but a certain brow of impatience rested over his eyes, as he walked fitfully around that rusty bench. His hands made random motions in the air, often the palms crumbling into each other or the hands making individual movements around the air. He seemed restless and although the reason for it I had well assumed was the absent damsel, the stupefying expressions went a little more than to express heartbreak. Sure enough, the freckled young woman arrived a little later with bulky luggage tugged to her back.

Both looked at each other for a while before breaking into expressions of delight and ecstasy, although in those joyful faces, there seemed to be hidden undisclosed words and emotions. They talked for a while, the arm of the young man around the neck of the woman (or whether it was over the woman on the bench?); giving the impression of yet another normal meet–up.

After a good thirty wandering rays later, they stood up together and unknowingly hugged each other, although without a cheerful smile. Suddenly they froze in their actions, staring at one another for a long time, again with a solemn expression upon their countenance. Did something sting up? I thought. They began to come nearer and stare intently towards one another, evidently looking right into the eyes of each other, closer and closer with their heads only advancing gradually, passionately and it was something different......... when a commotion on the other side of the park on that same cement track diverted my gaze. I saw another spiral of human confusion emerge with the moving of hands and shouting of words.

But, alas! When I looked back, the woman was gone from the scene while the young man sat on the bench, face down, elbows on the thighs, and the fingers interlocked into a fist. One second so close and another it looked as forlorn as a wet day.

It was several winds and rays later that the young man came out of his stance and walked groggily out of the park, into the mix of humans and words and sunshine. That day was pleasant and annoying. For one, I felt like grabbing the young man in my shade, I felt like doing it. Maybe my annoyance with the circumstances came in the way. That was the last that I saw of the freckled woman and the boy's smile. Occasionally, I noticed him in the park, hunched on a bench, looking dreamily into oblivion. From what I know of human expressions, it meant longing and nostalgia. Visibly emotion-draining.

When I said that I was unaware of the ending for all it is, it was true for the freckled woman but not for the young man, as he did not vanish from my observations in the park. Somewhere at some point in some way, he was present. Maybe because his facial hair grew as intently as the leaves of my branches, I gradually lost track of him. He became someone among anyone.

I am not being sentimental at this point as you would think. Perhaps a good ending would have given me that. But of all the decisions that I had taken in my career, the thought of understanding human relations of the opposite gender seemed the most draining and boring one. It proved so abrupt and rash, that I often messed up among the couples which I had seen the previous with the ones that were new and happy. So much so that I accepted the fact at the end for what it is: that humans are a crazy lot with undisclosed words.

The conversation-ender

"Are you going to eat that or not?" Mrs. Banerjee asked her husband, who sat nervously picking at his plate of steaming puris. As she said so, the expectant eyes of his daughter looked towards him. With a soft whisper, his ponytailed daughter chimed in, "Can I have it, Papa?" Mr. Bannerjee, out of his muse, gazed back at her with a wink and assuringly picked the hot puri, before placing it on the neighbouring plate. This gesture was awarded an annoyed look from the wife.

It was the dreaded phase of the writer's block that Mr. Banerjee had been suffering from, unable to pull anything out of his brilliant web of plots and heartbreaks. His last successful piece was a silent romance, but since then, his inspiration had vanished. Days went by but he couldn't get himself to hold a pen or kalam. Distraught and despondent, he couldn't bring himself to do anything else, it wouldn't suffice his love for the non-fiction and pages of texts and paragraphs–that included not being satisfied in the puris or the chole that his wife prepared every weekend, walking in the park nearby at dawn, or his favourite pastime, knitting--His daughter, a gleeful eight-year-old, took out a considerable amount of time, from her daily schedule of braiding and playing, to give him her mind.

"Perhaps, you can write about the sleeping beauty or the red riding hood," she would advise.

"They're already written," he would presume.

"I know. But I don't like it. Perhaps you can add some of your imagination in that,"

"Sweety, I'm not into fairytales," he was right, he wasn't.

For it was to weave out a stark reality of the prominent situations of the world that this twice–awarded narrator survived for and took pride in. He couldn't imagine something so ideal and far–fetched from reality to survive among the stout–minded and resolute souls of the era. But of course, when you talk of literature and books, it's never the moral that intrigues you, it's the story itself. And who was to say this? Not some invisible narrator but a timid and shy lad of nine or so whom he would meet under unsought circumstances. And not so literally, of course. He was nine.

It just so happened that when Mr. Banerjee once decided to not just sit dreamily curled up in his study, but get some fresh air from his window on the farther corner of the room, he witnessed an uncalled-for situation. The window offered a direct view of the bustling local market, where vendors, hawkers, and stores vied for the attention of pedestrians and shoppers.

On that sunny day, before one of the shops, a crowd of locals were gathered but instead of shopping, they seemed to bear that frustration of having their principles flouted or that authoritative anger over some felony.

Evidently the shop owner was the disdained one, venting his anger on the crowd after having his items stolen again, by some unrepented crook. The prominent fact of this situation which yearned for the writer's attention was that among the stolen items (as he was informed of later on), were a ballpoint pen that never leaked and a notepad. An odd choice for a petty thief.

Among the many perks of being an apt storyteller, one was that any situation which presented itself as unique or contradictory deserved Mr. Banerjee's attention–for with its weirdness it aimed for the popping of a new notion in the sticky web of his ideas.

So, he decided to wait for the unrepented crook to show his face again in the shop with the hopes of attaining some new insight on the absurdity that exists in the daily rigmarole of the common (Which he calculated would probably be after about a month or so, based on the pen's average lifespan). He even went as far as enquiring about the number of times it had happened so far, from the shopkeeper, after the crowd had dispersed. So, every day after a bland serving of lunch, he would sit in the local tea stall, a few metres away from the store, waiting for the crook. To steal another pen, which, for the record he had already paid for, and relieved the shop owner of the thought of having been duped. When the weather would settle into a gentle breeze and orange sky, he would depart glumly into his study. Such was Mr. Banerjee's curiosity about the whole affair that in ecstasy of the mission coming to fruition, he began stuffing up more from his plate than he had in the past few weeks.

"It's a mighty clingy affair. Wonder who would get as far as stealing to obtain a pen." he would talk to himself while savoring a morsel of rice mixed with spicy curry, and then chuckled to himself.

"It's to write, Papa," his daughter would presume, "Do you sit every afternoon drinking tea outside, for that? Isn't it boring?"

"For a fact, it isn't," he would say while grinning happily at her "Finish your curry" and ended the discussion with this.

One afternoon, as it happened thus, his dedication was awarded. As he was gulping down the sweet-hot tea of the tea seller, he noticed an expression of annoyance upon his person as he stirred milk on a pot over the fire.

"That boy's here," he replied to the question of his customer.

"That boy?" Mr. Banerjee claimed while pointing in the direction indicated by the tea seller, and he witnessed a slim–faced and dark-haired boy cautiously scrutinising his circumstances standing outside the shop. "Did he steal last time?" Mr. Banerjee asked the person.

"He did. I saw him running from there as fast as a wolf does." the person replied in the air of a detective, "Probably back for more,"

Mr. Banerjee did not hear the man's last remark, for he was staring intently at that boy, the supposed crook of his circumstances. But for what?

Before his suspicions could devour him, he stood up, placed his glass on the seat, and went in the direction of the shop in a casual way to not incite the boy's stead. Two dark brown eyes saw him approaching but before the little thief could act, the figure stopped and took out a pen from his back pocket before presenting it before the boy.

"For you," Mr. Banerjee added calmly to his gesture. The boy was silent and compliant.

"So, you like pens?" Mr. Banerjee said to his friend as they sat on the bench in the park. He had been able to win the boy's affirmation by his gesture and the fact that he had paid for all the stolen items. Yet he could not get the boy to speak.

As his gaze fidgeted in the grass and his arms remained stiff, the writer spoke up, "You like pens, don't you?"

No reply in advance.

"Or is it writing with them?" he added. Again, it went unanswered. But Mr. Banerjee held a firm resolve and started," Do you want to learn to write?"

To this, he was given a side eye from his companion. Yet it was enough for him to go on with his plan, for he had noticed some sincerity in the boy's eyes when he looked at it, small and stout, determined. That was enough motivation for him to continue his exchange.

"I can teach you to write if you want," he said reassuringly, to which the boy's arms loosened a little, but yet resistant.

"I am a writer, you know. So, you can trust me with that." Perhaps he should have begun the conversation with, it was the single–most unique character of him that somehow impressed the young soul as he looked up at him hesitantly but expectantly.

"You are?" the boy enquired meekly.

"Yes, I am. About a dozen so far. I hope to start writing soon after I overcome this writer's block"

"What's that?" the voice asked again. "What's what?"

"Writer's block?"

"Oh, it is.........well, I mean it is............ something when you cannot get any ideas about your next book,"

This sent his companion into a spiral of his imagination as he stared pensively toward the sky and the writer.

"You said you could teach me?" the boy continued after a lot of thought. "Yes, I can help you to write, if that's what you like," Mr. Banerjee replied confidently.

"Can we start now?"

"Oh! now?" his confidence began to dwindle.

"Yes, now" the boy assured him of his motive. With his dark-brown gaze. With the slightest hint of affirmation in the man's face, the boy took out a creasy notepad from his pocket where he had kept it crumpled. This gave the man a heads-up on the boy's demeanour and the task he had taken at hand (something he was impressed enough to continue).

Over the next few days, they went with the knowledge of the alphabets, which the boy was sufficiently good at. With outstanding penmanship. Later Mr. Banerjee decided to start with sentences. He would teach his student to write an introduction or give him a paragraph to copy from one of his books. On some occasions, it was a paragraph from one of his books and sometimes he would pick one from his daughter's innumerable fairy tales.

The few days spared him the knowledge that the boy was a fast-learner and the fact that he could well write his full name: Dheeraj.

Once when he did finish writing his introduction, Mr. Banerjee realised after looking at it that he had never asked the boy about his family,

"Do you live with someone? Dheeraj?" he asked once after a daily writing session at the park.

The boy remained silent for a time gathering up the words to speak of his family, "I live alone," he replied demurely after a silence, "But I do have a brother,"

"Oh, where is he? Does he lives with you?" Mr. Banerjee enquired. But it went unanswered that day, as the only clarity he could regarding the situation was that his bright student did not wish to speak of it......or rather keep it a secret. Both are different and probable.

Further into this daily routine of teaching, Mr. Banerjee obtained the familiarity to reveal the cause of his visits, to his family. This, for one, was because his daughter took after her father.

"What is it that you're doing, Papa?" she would curiously point. "What do you mean?" he would reply.

"You started visiting the park daily? Did you get over the block?"

"I'm afraid not," the father replied with a sigh, "It's something else I'm doing," and tried to end it.

"What is it?" and the questions would continue.

One day after dinner he decided to end his daughter's curiosity with a final revelation, "I'm teaching someone,"

"Who? Is it a boy?" "Yes, a nine-year-old,"

"You've started taking tuitions?" his wife poked from the kitchen. "Not that. It's because I want to teach,"

"Oh.... is he good?" his daughter asked. "Quite a learner,"

"What are you teaching him?" "To write," he replied. His daughter smirked a little at this imaginary student for having to write at this age and his father understood the ridicule "He was passionate about the writing, so we started with it. Later on, I may give him some books to read,"

"If he can write, he can surely read it. Doesn't he?" "Yes, he can," the writer claimed proudly.

Only a few weeks with this boy and he was as hearty as a muffin. When he first saw him at the market, he knew for one that the waiting and paying was not a waste after all. The boy's eyes narrated it, his passion and dedication and hard work. His brilliance. But for what?

Another version of the curiosity confronted the writer late one night in his study, as he sat pondering over the recent incidents. With another resolute pair of eyes, he decided to satisfy this desire for clarity. Dheeraj's determined eyes fueled his desire for answers. 'He seemed pretty sane and able-bodied to attend a school.........or was there something more?' he brimmed over the blurry thought.

"Do you go to school?" the teacher enquired with his student on one of their sessions.

The boy answered with a nod of affirmation. "So, you get to write there, don't you?"

Again, a nod.

"Dheeraj, why are you learning from me then?" This came in rather an offended tone from the man, but he did not intend to question the boy about his choices.

"What do you expect from me then?" he corrected himself and spoke with a much-softened tone towards the boy's solemn expression.

"What do you want to learn?" he re-corrected himself.

After a moment of silence, the boy replied meekly in his shy nature, "To write,"

The writer was puzzled for a bit at having to hear the same reply. He had a stark proof of this desire to write, but why then from him? The problem seemed to devour him, but in time he got the right query to counter-balance it.

"Write what?" he queried his student, "Something specific, is it?"

The boy looked up at his teacher and replied with a sense of achievement, “A book, I have an idea,”

Among all of the other possibilities, Mr. Banerjee could not comprehend the reason for the boy's desire to write. A book, it is.

“Oh, you want to be an author?” he said, smiling and chuckling at the young visionary.

“I want to write a book,” the boy repeated.

The shock of the revelation wore out after that night, as Mr. Banerjee realised the gravity of the situation. Doubts of instability and incapability shrouded him. He never speculated the fact from his perspective, how did he become one?

He was sure it was not taught to him. Just the passion was enough for a person to weave a new story and a part of his creation. He did not want to disappoint the boy and tell him to move along alone on this journey. So, he did what sought him well. He decided to help the boy, hear his ideas, and do the utmost in his powers to make him an author.

Boisterously, he went up the next day at 5 in the park with a satchel and saw his friend reading sincerely at their designated spot by the tree.

“You like sweets?” he asked but before the boy could reply, the man held out a pack of barfis in front of him, opened it, and urged him to try it.

While the boy gobbled up the sweets, the writer looked intently at him, preparing a set of questions in his brain to satisfy.

“Dheeraj, you want to become an author, don’t you?” “Yes.” came the reply.

"Then you can tell me your ideas. I will help you to write a story." "Won't you teach me how to write it?"

"Dheeraj," Mr. Banerjee began with a serious tone,

"I cannot teach you how to write a book, it should come from you. But I can teach with the grammar and sentences."

"What is it other than that? A story?"

"Dheeraj, a story is much more than a narrative.... it's about capturing an emotion, an expression and weaving it into a narrative, it's special"

"Emotion?" the boy mouthed.

"You have your ideas to start with if you want,"

"But..................." the boy fumbled, attracting the man's gaze, "The ideas are not mine."

"Whose is it?"

"My brother," the boy narrated,

"He used to narrate a story to me when I was five. I didn't have any books to read, so he created new stories for me. They were good."

"Is it your brother's idea? Where is he?"

"I don't know. He lives in the hospital, some government one." "He lives there?"

"He has polio, so he needs to be there" the boy finally clarified and was met with an empathetic look from his mentor.

"Your brother..........how old?"

"Fourteen running," "Oh, he likes to write,"

"Before the polio, all he did was write on his notepad."

The day's revelations unfolded strangely. He realised the cause of the absurd circumstances, his getting to teach a boy who desired to be an author. It was the innocence of his brother's stories that drove this little boy into fulfilling his brother's on his behalf. Everything seemed to come in place for him at this point, but for one which the writer felt compelled to address.

"Do you have the interest?" he asked the boy with a pat on his thighs. "I like these stories........not the other bulkier ones."

"So how will you write your book........without interest? It will slowly drain you out, and it will affect the storyline ," the writer claimed though not to the boy but to himself, as he was sure the boy would not perceive it as such . He would not understand the fact that a story is not just something to be done with. It is to be dealt with. The writer's despondence in this situation collected over his brows went over to the other side through his clear eyes. For a split second, the garden changed into his study room, and a younger Bannerjee was seen scribbling words on paper from the glow of a lamp while the owls hooted and the town snored. "A writer's mind is made to deal with his stories.......without it, the story loses its essence.

The man's further talk was interrupted when his student took out a piece of paper from his pocket, a crumpled one, and offered it to the man. When he uncrumpled the paper, Mr. Banerjee saw a writing in black ink among the creases: The Prince of Winterland.

On the other side was a story, a small one but a funny one, as he would know later.

"Can you write that story? You're a writer," the boy added to his gesture and looked gratefully at the man, who was pondering upon his next action or............ reaction. But he couldn't bring himself to reply. For whatever reasons.

It was only after Mr. Banerjee settled himself in his study for the day that glanced over at the single-lined paper. He began mind-reading it and smiled. Chuckled. Grinned. And mused: A story has a soul, a twin of the writer's, an essence of the pen-pushing.

"Papa? Are you coming to eat?" his daughter enquired while standing at the threshold of the half-opened door.

"Yes, I am," her father replied willingly. "In a bit,"

"What are you reading?" The obvious question came. "Oh, nothing," Mr. Banerjee said.

"Is it good?" "It's funny,"

"Oh, then you should write about it," "I'll think about it,"

"Ok, can I take your puri by that time?" "Oh, sweet," Mr. Banerjee replied to her daughter's trick.

For the information, he did not think about it. He wrote about it. It was all he could do. Write.

The Serial Cleaner

Unless you are some absent-minded daydreamer like our protagonist–Andy–you would probably not like the idea of changing venues around the year, doing just one boring, unskillful, and a terrifying premonition of a job: sweeping. Around the clock, twenty-four seven. But it did prove satisfactory and settling (for some hidden reason) to this tall, slim, and bony figure who had perhaps the only hobby of observing other than swinging the mop, in the enclosures of the biggest zoo in town.

Before this, he had a whole barrel of experience in sweeping the floors of schools, hospitals, auditoriums, and roads in different locations. Perhaps his lengthy resume was so satisfactory that the head of the cleaning staff hired him without a spill of skepticism or regret. For obvious reasons, it had come as a surprise to his counterparts when they were informed of his smartness and prowess–which he had done owing to his laziness to secure a decent job. So, till that particular day in that sultry summer month, upon the bear enclosure, he wiggled with his mop towards every nook and cranny of the wide space of grass and rubble, whistling a tune he had heard from a roadside tea stall.

Before him, far above the whole territory of the mammal, a wide array of spectators stood gazing and peeking towards a makeshift cave, hoping for a glimpse at the majestic animal. They poked their head over the white railing of the area, custom-made for adventurers to not slip off it and fall into the enclosure. Until perhaps you can get in through the side door meant for the cleaning staff. Towards which the tall figure now trudged tiredly. He had wasted a little of his soul in wiggling that he felt a slight spasm erupting from one of his calf muscles.

So, in view of using the little leisure he had from his chores, he went to the area covered by the shade from one of the trees of the enclosures. Stooping against the cement wall, he began observing the general public. Around the zoo. Clinging into their shoes and donning their personality. Assuming and observing.

Red-haired and booted, perhaps a foreigner.

Grey-haired and slim waist, perhaps a fitness enthusiast. White-haired and protruding belly, must be retiring.

Likewise, he had done so at schools, hospitals, and alleyways. Children, doctors, miscreants, he had seen them all.

Not suspiciously, but curiously, gratefully, dreamily. In the hold of those little observations, he may have realised a non-existent part of his being, one which never came to fruition or never expressed upon him . Through these observations, he glanced at the infinite possibilities lived through the flesh of others.

As he sat wondering over these, his eyes caught the benign attention of a man–tall, fair, smartly-dressed–bending over the white railing, back towards his observer. The fairer one looked at his watch from time to time hinting that he was waiting for someone. Thankfully, the lanky figure of a woman came in attendance to this, which then gracefully started their conversation. They chatted for a little while with the man's occasional pin-points towards the cage.

Except for the fact that it was not the tall, charming personality of the man that devoured Andy's attention, but the simple recollection that he had seen him before. In this place. With someone else. To what depth this matter reached, Andy was well unknown of. Yet from that smarty-pants sector of his mind, there came a voice yearning to reach the depth. Just because the man he saw was the man he had seen.

So cruel is the intellect, that it does not let a man sweep till the remainder of his life.

Was it to continue at this pace? And is there something to be done about it? He couldn't think much, for quite sharply came the nudgy remarks of the burly manager, from behind. The matter slept then and there.

Not for long though!

It was quickly in a matter of days that our vigilant sweeper met the dashing persona of the stranger once again, with another woman, over another enclosure. How was it that he was to resist the recurrent urges of his mind from looking over? After all, who comes in a jacket to a zoo?

He set a deal with his conscience to count the number of times the stranger had caught his attention over the course of one month. Then he may share it with his superiors (if they care to listen). It did turn out that as the numbers increased, more vibrant and vehement visuals of the man seemed to circle the enclosures. Near the tiger's, by the shade of the tree, in the cafeteria. Everywhere and forever!

Maybe he's being over-sensitive about it, Andy once thought, placing his chin in his cupped palms. It had not been a month, but he had already seen the man more than a dozen times. With different people. And no same redhead even surfaces after an hour. Over-conscious and insecure, he went to his superior, Mr. Jackson, to discuss the matter over.

"There's this man" the sweeper began, "He keeps showing up in the zoo repeatedly,"

"So," came the obvious reply.

"Well, I bet you don't visit a local zoo that many times, on weekdays.

The bald and crooked shape of a man rose from his chair, and sat near his employee over the desk, facing him as it is. As if with a mixed feeling of emotional trepidation and turmoil, he says "So you think he's the killer,"

"What? No...wait, what killer?" Andy mouths with a shaking.

"Well, I thought you had the whole front page of the morning paper memorised," with a chuckle came the words. "It's a very nasty affair, you know. With headlines and all that stuff." this with disgust.

The word had a shocking reaction on Andy's nerves as he could only stare open-mouthed at his superior, whiskers trembling and skin whitening to sawdust. Killing. Killer. He was too dejected to even think about them. Besides, his earlier interpretations and inclinations towards the stranger's presence did not stem from any criminal angle, but rather a sensible one.

Perhaps you would say it overthinking at best. But for him, it erupted from pure common sense. He had his share of hospitals and other business venues where men of purpose collect in elegant crowds to talk and be heard. Even while vacating there's a purpose behind all that we do. The mojito for a new experience and the bubble bath for a tactile touch of elegance and Luxor.

In short, he had developed a knack for determining where people fit or the purpose of their stay. Thanks to his non-concentrated job. So having a man without an acute purpose to the place may have rigged his nerves for that. His superior would seriously take it otherwise, though.

"Sweep along, gentleman. It's none of your business to meddle with the purposes of others. Do what you are meant to do." with a touch of authority that sounded more like arrogance.

Having been rejected by the manager, he went about his business. His urge was still unfulfilled and unsatisfied. Not for long.

The next time he saw the stranger in a beige-coloured jacket and navy-blue pants, talking to another man of the same height and hair, he overheard.

“........the lion is feisty and strong.” the conversation continued. “But only for the prey. When a predator meets a predator it’s both of them that are in danger.”

“The wolf?”

“Oh, he’s the watcher from the hills above.” “So, he only watches,”

“He observes and defeats.” “Can he be defeated?”

“Only with another brain, I heard.” this in a compliant tone.

The conversation was cut short for the unwelcomed listener. As he saw the two men in a position of walking, he went the other way. Thinking about the lion and the wolf. But the predator?

His amateurish attempts at spying upon the stranger had been taken into consideration, however. After a few days of whistling, Andy was called into the manager’s office. He entered through the door.

And saw two men sitting on opposite sides of the centre table. One is his bald superior. Other his slim-faced stranger. One smirking. One grinning. It's not a good one.

As he advanced and stood next to the seated stranger, the gentleman stood and pushed his right hand forward in a handshake to the sweeper.

“Hello, Andy. It’s Officer Barnes. Mill Bay Centre.” His voice had the dexterity of politeness and authority. And Andy accepted the hand adding, “Hello, Officer.”

"Is this the man you're tailing?" the superior enquired from the other side impatiently. Andy afforded a nod to this.

"Well, for clarity," the officer began,

"I am looking over the case of Jude Art's murder down at Millbay." "That unknown killer case, is it?" Andy enquired confidently. He had plodded through the newspapers before it.

"Yes, unknown it remains. We got a lead of the culprit here somewhere." "Okay."

"We were investigating the same. It seems that the killer has a distinct practice of finding his victims from this place."

"Okay." and a gulp down the throat.

"So, Andy, since you have such a keen eye for disruption, it'd be better if you help us in finding the culprit. Is that better?"

"Okay," a wave of amusing anxiety disrupts his nerves one more time, expressing itself with a grin.

The handsome personality of the inspector bid a reassuring smile to each of his neighbours, before rushing out in a dutiful hurry. Andy was assured at best. Not long before the stinging remark-y gaze of the manager fell upon his attention. And he rushed outside.

.... a change of scenario.

A tall, fair and brown-haired officer in a jacket and vest walks hurriedly through the crowd of bewildered locals and a handful of daring cronies. Getting past the police tape, he stops before the stark-dead figure of a man-limbs spread out, eyes staring at the heavenly ceiling of the world with a mouth open in a mid-scream sense. Beside him, stooped over the body was a woman, with black hair in a white overcoat.

She looks starkly into the man's directionless eyes, then his face, shoulders, and overalls. His neck.

"What have we got, Cathy?" the comrade slips into his question. "Strangulated in a way," she remarks in a dutiful tone. "Not with hands, though"

"Not with hands? What is it?"

She looks up and over the question examining it with the keenness and dexterity similar to the crime. And continues while pointing to the victim's orange-reddish texture of the neck,

"You see these here, it's straight and across a certain pattern. Perhaps the man was pinned down to the floor with a stick on his neck. And then...." She let her voice drift along the complex anatomy of the lifeless remains.

"And then, with the stick, he broke the bone,"

The comrade gathered the comfort to hear of the crime committed, for it was the sixth week and the sixth body. No clue as to the whereabouts.

He frustratingly slammed a nearby tree hard and pondered over the unknown killer's existence.

"Barns," the young doctor began, "... in the same way..." "Oh, I know it. Don't tell me about it. It's been weeks so far." "What about the lead?"

"Patrolling the area, and beyond that too. Even got the help of some employees,"

"Officer Barns," a voice said from afar. "Mikhail?"

"Well, we've got the identity." the other officer began confidently,

"As you see, the victim's a redhead, Mark Prady, a tourist from Germany. Had a two-week layover in Morstan."

"The itinerary?" That is the layout of his journey.

"A water park, restaurant, fishing and then..............." trailing behind for a little, the officer continued, "The zoo," and finished grimly.

Officer Barns moved fitfully from one tree to another and back, gathering all the essential data he had so far. Six weeks. Six tourists. All had the same last destination of visit. But different places to die. No ties. One killer.

It was stupid and brilliant, he thought while standing over the lifeless body of Mark Prady.

"Call the family. Leave me alone," he ordered harshly.

Perhaps the grimness of the evening had been setting upon him (or was it the case?) Either way, he looked pleadingly at the body, chatting with the unknown killer in his head.

"I'll catch you." "You won't get far."

"This is not the best one yet."

"A stick for a weapon. Pretty low-cost, I say."

Before he could continue further, the endless flashes of camera light disturbed his train of thoughts.

He looked behind to gaze at a crowd of reporters before the tape, in dire need of an update.

The comrade let out a sigh of annoyance and sped ahead. “Mr. Barns? What is the update for tonight?” one reporter began. “Dead redhead......in bold” came the reply.

“What is with the killer? Have you searched enough?”

“We will continue with the search,” the officer replied, “But as of now, the wolf’s won, it seems”

“And the weapon?” The question came erupting from one of the mouths and signified the importance of the day ahead and afar. With several others from the crowd. Forever in direct harmony with human nature. Chaos and death. Go hand in hand.

Three words to end: stick. broom. zoo.

The Nightmarer

Year 2187,

In regard to the present situation which I find myself in, it started with normal circumstances in place. I had gone about my daily routine of desk-typing in the sunny hours among the cloudy vales of Cloudville, spending the silver hours gliding over the artificial lights one megacity after another. Embracing the cottony sky, racing with the razor-sharp wind. All went well till then. Perhaps it had to be pristine or else I wouldn't have taken the burden of performing my neighbouring cloudie's work after he fell sky-sick. To give a brief, I am no human and Cloudville is not something any pedestrian will ever experience in its lifetime. Situated over a sky-white area of humongous clouds, it is the abode of the sleep-diggers and the horror of the thunder-clouds, who are as dark as the clouds are white. As you plod ahead, you will get a brief of our work as well. So, plod along.

I had done it before. The calming down anxious teenagers and cradle-crawling babies.

Like an embrace from a candy-sweet and velvety-soft apparition, I could put a clingy toddler into the world of lollies and hugsies. The small human slept, crumpled, sucking his thumb and halting his wiggly-legs in mid-air. The smile of a century rested on their supple expression, which was comforting. "I will meet you in the dreams, little one," I would whisper in the silence towards the crib while making my way through the tiny slit in the window and into the glow-y night-life beyond it. That was probably fifty years ago. My itinerary for that night was one destination. Where I was headed. To a red-painted sloped-roofed two-storey house among other colourful homes. I should have had no business with the family, had not it been for their nine-year-old's aversion to peaceful dreaming. That's what I was going for and that's what several of my counterparts were unable to perform.

You might point out how could one sleep without dreaming or imagining. As far as the explanation regarding that goes, this polite three-foot hadn't had a single vision of soft cloudy-liked dreams, but nightmares and dark places to the point where she could sit legs-folded on her bed at three in the morning waiting for the clock to strike out.

Perhaps the thunder clouds were at play for this. Those nasty ill-looking grey-coloured monstrous bundles of vapour won't tire out of spreading their nightmarish tactics to the whole of the population. Perhaps it was their sinister ideas that brought about such a failure in the field of dreams.

The weather that day was practically wholesome with the first summer shower in close proximity. The sky was outlined with white bushes and circlets of light. I flew a little low nearer to where the heat embraced my neck and the endless chirping of nightlings reached one's deepest thoughts and motives.

Through the nightlife and into a more peaceful surrounding near a slumbering neighbourhood, I made my way down to the destination, where the wind is directed. Looking the shade of a dark red from all the absence of actual light, the house stood as gloomily as it could be among a queue of other similar architecture. The windows were emitting the moonlight out into the front street. I made my way to the top right one, curtained and barred (quite a cold welcome) but the other one was a little warmer, just curtained slightly, leaving a slit to see through in the middle.

The sight was there. I peeped into the glow of the room connecting it. A low light was powered from one end of the wall. Its glow fell on the opposite side of the bed and a figure seemed to be wrapped among the bed sheet and blanket. At this point, it was probably the thoughts of going inside the room that disturbed my concentration.

How do I get in?

Well, simple, I searched for a hole. A tiny one would have done. A see-through. From some old unfinished reparations. The chimney was the last resort, in certain cases. But in this case, luck was the wind of my surroundings, helping me to locate that discreet detail among the window railings. I wouldn't explain the mechanics behind the existence of that tiny little wear among the rubber of the sliding window, but it did somehow find its way in the years. So, I focused on it and in the next second, the faulty glow of the low-power bulb seemed to cuddle me in an unwelcoming reunion.

From the presence of a stacked set of old and used notebooks on the desk and spread-out sketch-pens near it, I deduced this room to be the right one. With the nine-year-old. It was nearly midnight, but as I tried to unlock the state that the crumpled figure was in, it seemed to look back. With two large dark-green eyes, undead and reasonable. Not long after, the whole shape of the figure came into place, from the warmth of the cosy covers. I noticed two large eyes, a wheatish-coloured hue for skin colour, a blunt nose, visible ears and long silky hair wound tightly and gratefully into two ponytails that curled ever so beautifully from the shoulders of my nightmare-dreamer.

And it smiled, though not with the childishness of a nine-year-old, but with the discreteness of a ninety-year-old. I thought for a fact about whether I was not the unwelcomed and unknown guest this time. Bearing no thought to these distractions, as the possessor of those bright eyes looked up at me, I smiled back.

"Hello, child," the usual conversation-beginner. "How are you today? Great, I presume." I began by stooping near the bedside.

The child grinned back.

"What would you like to dream about today? Perhaps, a formidable win against a bully," I suggested sheepishly.

The child focused her gaze on this, at me. More so than towards me.

Her vision intensified further and in those two bright spots of her figure, I watched my image. Hazy and unformed.

"Perhaps a new skill. How about swimming?" I continued fitfully with the same gentleness and poise that I had shown to folks half the size of this reflective figure.

"Perhaps...." I halted as I noted the first signs of incoming words from her supple rosy lips. It formed in a kind of oval shape, sucking in air and finally letting it out.

"Home." It said those plain four letters. The warmer reference to the house.

It caught me in that spiral of doubts and dreams. A home? Where, if not here? Why? I let out my dumb-foundedness at this with a slow grin.

And enquired further, "Where exactly do you plan to go, my child?" "Home," came the reply.

"Where is it?" I asked.

"It's..." she halted, "Where I lived, near the backwaters." "Oh, so you want to dream about it?"

She nodded dutifully, but before she could lose my attention, the lips spoke up, "But I want you to come with me."

So sweetly and sincerely it escaped from those lips that I readily found myself in a pickle. The situation in the beginning.

Presently, I was scaling the perimeter of the room, in deep thought regarding the consequences of future actions. The girl, as it were, had left her blanket and was swinging her legs from the bedside.

"Can I do so? What if I get stuck? What are the side effects of this? Is it even possible?" I shouted these words from behind my vision and into that dark spot where no one could hear it.

After much pacing, I stopped near the clumsy desk, facing the girl, looking curiously at her, reasoning out the reason for her request.

“I’m scared,” the girl quickly spoke, as though sensing my agitation. “It’s quite dark in there.”

I did not wish to lower her spirits by asking about the reason for the darkness, so I tried to ease the predicament.

“I’ll... try,” the words jousted out.

In the next few minutes, I took the girl's palms and thought hard. Then told the girl to think hard. These minutes were unknown and important and I could have sensed the uncertainty from the pulse of my dreamer’s hands.

They didn’t turn into hours. The minutes.

In a split second, as I raised my vision, the atmosphere had changed. For the worse.

Grime and soot surrounded it. Dilapidation breathed on its shoulders. All in all, the house was the epitome of abandonment and left-outness. What was it? My companion smelled of the answer. She breathed a large pump of air. Beyond the entrance door, a creaky wooden corridor ran, filled with the putrid smell of rotten furniture. A small staircase was at one end and opposite to it a wall. Not any wall. But the sum of all the memories that confounded the settlement. Pictures and portraits. Photo frames bordering it. About a dozen or more of them hung from the sooty board of plaster and dried paint. It breathed itself of olden times. Not much older, though.

Considering the girl's age, it wouldn't have been more than a decade old. But then time does wait for none. And dirt does not even take one's breath to settle on one's memories. As the circumstances provided. Perhaps it did not take me long to realise that it really provided some kind of nostalgia for the little girl. From the way she caressed the dirt with her fingertips or glanced wistfully at the darkness, lost in dreamy thoughts, pleasant ones, for her lips edged upwards occasionally.

It was her home. And I sensed it.

As I started searching my surroundings with her, it quickly came to place. All the nightmares and all. Perhaps a trauma had been at play with this girl's dreams igniting the nightmares. I feared the worst-case scenario.

Is she an orphan?

Are her parents dead? Does she not have anyone?

My chain came to a jerk as the girl motioned me towards the wall of memories. With all the pictures. I raced towards it and within the light of my positivity, the old times came to surface. I relished them and revelled in them with the little girl to cheer her spirits.

There was one with a bearded man, the little girl at his strong shoulders. They laughed in the greenery of their surroundings.

Another saw the little one racing with a boy on a road. The photo adjacent to it provided another of their games. The boy lay triumphantly on the ground and the girl sat haughtily over him.

They're siblings! A cheerful guess turned into a dreadful one.

Another one saw a lake with fishing rods stung into it. Three to count for the man, the boy and the girl.

The last one I saw before I turned my gaze towards the girl was a family photo of four.

A typical happy family. The man. The boy. The girl. A woman.

Then I turned towards my companion. She had followed my gaze to the family photo. She stared at it for uncountable minutes. Dreamily. Gratefully. Pleadingly. Finally, happily. A sliding of those fingertips through the frames swept the age-old grime and brightened the colour of the times long been painful memories for the girl. Then it became her pride. And her nightmare.

In the next few minutes, she did something unmistakably weird for her position. Flinging her hands to the wall, she discreetly unhooks the family photo from its nail, before placing it between her arm and waist and winking at the distraught figure of me.

In case you might think, how I am perceived by others, it's usually the mirror image of the dreamers. But as luck would put it, some can see me with such intensity and greed, it would right away replace the mask of deceit.

I don't quite recollect the final moments of our exchange. My invisible blood was getting spent by the minute in that darkness. Somehow, I just focused on the obstinate little soul-suckers of those eyes, perhaps seeking for permission. A request. A desire.

Oh, how I love that. That desire seeming to express itself more vibrantly in kids hit me hard and deeply. And in that instant, it pointed towards the object between the hand and waist of the little girl.

The picture. Can I keep it? It seemed to plead.

My mind was filled with thoughts of acceptance and encouragement devoid of loathe and disapproval. I did not know whether we could take it

, though.

It could not come out. So after a few clumsy minutes of silence, we joined hands, beginning to come out of the realm. As I try to recollect those few moments of word exchange between the shabby home and the lighted house, the girl did something that I don't usually care about. Nonetheless, it was prudent and bold.

A closure of the circumstances.

That's what it's called, as I came to know of it later. An explanation of the circumstances which led to the execution of the respective behaviours on her part. And mine too. That too with a lengthy sentence, before she went to sleep and I to heaven.

"I like my aunt very much, but." the girl began, "I don't want the nightmares to stop."

Those words continued to ring in my cloudy recollections, as I watched for the last time that night, clinging to a picture of a family of four, but it wasn't the same one. The photo of her and a woman and a hairy spaniel, seated beside them.

"Her aunt..." the same one in the dusty photo, which I held in my palms. Glancing to and fro from one to another and the girl. That was the whole scenario of my first dream job after nearly fifty years, ending in something unforgettable.

Now that I view these in chronological order, it doesn't seem too pitiful or droll. All thanks to the closure. As to the picture, I still keep it at my desk among the many whitish and volatile cubicles. It still bears the dust of the abandoned home.

Still, it sets itself apart as a fervent reminder of the futility and magic there is in being clingy. Sometimes the image of the little dreamer flashes in my thoughts clinging on to the photo or something regarding the happy ending. It reminds me that not all has changed with this species after so many decades. In the blend of artificial lights and with a much-layered persona in public, they still are the product of their primitive ancestors. Foolish and curious. Emotional and dreamy.

Small snippet of the nightmare:

A family of three on a car, going over a highway. It is evening dark and a sunless horizon stretches from all extremes. Dark into their seats. The girl plays with her doll, and the boy sees into the passing environment. The father's a little dreamy and absent-minded, it seemed. Suddenly from the front, visible in the windshield is a speck of light, growing bigger by the second. And in the span of one grooming of her shoulder hair, the little nightmarer experiences a sudden burst of energy in her seat, seeming to blow her off and put her to sleep. But she didn't sleep at that time. It wasn't time for the eternal slumber. Of course, the same wouldn't have been articulated for her brother and father.

The first time she saw them after waking up was the last time she saw them ever, they were operated on by several off-white and transparent medical thingies, living and nonliving. The wait, the faces and their silence , particular to the one she experienced in her ramshackle of a house. All but one that still persisted in the surgical atmosphere was the smile drooping from her father's chapped lips. Maybe it made its way through his wrecked system on seeing her, standing and staring. Such was the merriment in that dried smile, that she couldn't resist smiling back. To smile forever in her nightmares.

The Night with a Stranger

The street lights had gone off.

The road was quiet and spooky. But not so much as to prevent any nocturnal whispers.

There in the darkness, she saw the glow emanating out of a building, white and creamy, it sprayed on the road ahead.

The sign: Quacky Flavours, heightened the girl's attention. She hastily but calmly made her way through the desolate surroundings towards the light. The broken doll was secured in her right hand.

Inside the shop, behind the display panel for a thousand creamy flavours of ice cream, stood a young man, wiping the counter, whistling an out-of-place melody and wistfully looking at the colours on the four walls around it.

He was so immersed in his rendition, that he did not notice the seating of a little stranger on a bench overlooking the street. As he diverted his attention to the third wall, bearing the glass window, the little girl made a wave of musical appreciation, earning the man an appropriate scare.

“Do you have chocolate, sir?” the little girl asked politely before the man could voice his enquiry.

And the man complied with a friendly nod and the acquisition of a scoop from one of the boxes.

“Bowl or cone?” the man asked, raising an eyebrow in surprise.. “Cone,” came the reply.

In the matter of ten seconds, the man was beside the little girl, serving the double-scoop cone and glancing at the state of his customer. A bright yellow dress, a colourful hair band across the burgundy hair, with a pony at the back. And of course, the shaggy look of the broken doll, on the table. He had never seen her.

“Are you from here?” the first question. No answer.

“Where are your parents, dear?” the second question, with more deliberation. No answer.

“What’s your favourite flavour?” A friendly but idiotic one. Yet this invited the girl’s cherry-eyed gaze.

“They’re sleeping,” the girl replied casually as the man began towards the counter.

“And you came here alone?” “Yes. They’ll come to get me,”

“You shouldn’t be here. Where’s your home?” Again, no reply. Signalling the departure of the man with bent shoulders to the counter

“Can I draw?” the girl asked while munching on the last part of the cone. The man, as weary as he was, reasoned on the time being a little ungodly for leisure.

Yet he wasn’t going to let that make the girl rebellious. “Of course,” he said," do you have your colours?"

“Yes, of course,”

There was no backing down, so the next half an hour saw the girl racing her pencils through the white sheet of paper in front of her, occasionally having a careful look at the man, behind the counter. The atmosphere was pencil-sharpening and ticking and barking all along.

The shop had overstayed its timings by the time the girl found a reason to get up from her bench and walk to the counter before the man, sulking on a magazine.

“What’s your name?”

The man, taken aback by the sudden questioning, coughed and itched, before regaining his stance and replying, “Diego,”

The girl giggled and joked about it being a cartoon character’s name, “I didn’t know anyone had that name,” the girl added to her routine of giggling.

“Well, I do. And my parents know,” the man replied in defense.

“Do you like it?” the girl questioned further before showing a mix of pencil drawings on the white sheet to the man.

It was a giant elephant carrying a family man, a woman, and a girl. “Are they your family?”

“Yes, of course,”

“Well, where are they going?” added as a joke. “I don’t know,”

The clock then ticked a noisy twelve, gaining two pairs of eyes. “It’s late,” the man remarked.

"It's time," the girl interfered.

A change of scenario:

The car was upturned and fuming, all broken glass and red liquid all over on the place. In the dead of the night, it would have been the grim reaper that came out of that mangled apparition of a vehicle. Instead, a middle-aged, brown-haired man paced his way clumsily out of one of the broken glasses, crawling and trudging. Hungry for life and the living. He invests his energy in walking upright and going over for help, as the two mangled pieces of steel and fuel interest the grim reaper. Before meandering off, he takes one look back at the two mangled frameworks of cars, one his own and the other bearing a white stripe on the dashboard.

The man, hobbling and walking crookedly in the dark, unwelcoming street sees a shop on the far side of the block, glowing. Relieved for the time, he trudged towards it, crookedly with a palm over the right knee. Limping and gradually approaching. His walk is cut short by a person coming from his destination, briskly advancing towards him.

He realised then that he was bleeding from his temples, a red streak across his nose, and the pain in his knee was heightening with every step. So much so that by the time the stranger neared a margin, his legs lost grip, his eyes consciousness and he fell right into the arms of the stranger, Diego.

Back to the first scenario:

"Can you look outside?" a question erupted. "Why?" Diego questioned.

"To see if my parents have come or not,"

"Will they come now?"

A nod and he stood up from his seat and crossed the counter, went straight for the entrance. Running a keen eye outside, he glanced into the darkness in the light of his shop, towards the grey buildings ahead and about. Suddenly, he noticed a man walking gradually towards his shop, more so than it is, limping towards him.

Fearing for the man, he briskly walks to him only to have him in his grip by the time he reaches him. The stranger looked pale and red streaks of blood were visible around his traumatic expressions.

"Sir?"

The man looked for consciousness but there was not any in the unconscious soul. He tidily brought the man to his shop and placed him on a sack of cushions behind the counter. He noticed the girl sitting on a bench in the corner, looking distraught and despondent. He did not involve her.

After a quick call to the ambulance, Diego rechecked the man's pulse and found it beating out of his veins. He brought on a first-aid kit from the back of the shop, using it to aid the stranger. His knee was hurt, so it was bandaged on a temporary basis. His pulse took shape and before long it awoke the stranger into consciousness.

As the sirens of the red van filled the humid air with anticipation, so did the man's narration. On his way to the hospital in the ambulance, the middle-aged stranger gave the shop owner a friendly smile.

"You saved my life."

The owner could only smile back.

Before he could leave, he grabbed onto the hand of another of the paramedics, saying,

“What about the other car?”

The young paramedic looked down and politely nodded in disapproval, “I’m sorry, sir,”

“The girl, too?” the question erupted out of the bleeding mouth of the survivor, as he was taken to the hospital.

In these goings on, a little girl sat invisibly among the infinite benches in the stall, her eyes were watery and red with a hint of a wound near the head.

“Mamma.... Papa.”

The clock rang one by the time the shop owner could regain his posture around the shop. He read the clock, checked for the lights, and searched for the girl around the shop.

Except that she was absent from the benches.

Nowhere near the counter or the window or the cushions, gone. Leaving her belongings on the bench she sat on earlier.

Diego curiously went near the belongings noticing the broken doll, the white sheet, and the pencils.

The last visual on the sheet had the elephant changed into a car, an upturned one.

The night faded into the moonlight as the tears of the little one changed to red streaks, fighting their way through her cheeks. From the upturned car bearing a white stripe on the dashboard, it sped off to heaven.

A friend in need

The stream flowed powerfully against the stones and boulders on either surface of it, reflecting the milky-blue sky and housing some of the longest-living creatures of the forest. Perhaps Arun was holding one that day as he searched frantically for a certain something in the wilderness, starting with the stream as his reference point.

He had rummaged through the muddy dirt of the bank and across the boulder, taking count of every little stone. When he chanced upon a creature, mistaking it for a hollow shell and holding it for view in his dirty hands.

"Hey, there, little buddy" he politely said to the sleepy-eyed turtle, "Perhaps you may have something I have been looking for,"

He gently jutted the turtle, earnestly trying to prevent his shrinking in defence. Before placing it on a shaded portion of the bank, covered by a large boulder.

"I'll search for it somewhere else. Sleep tight."

Suddenly from below the cold bottoms of the stream, there emerged something which shook the general rhythm of the water.

"If you don't plan to do something, at least help me," Arun said to the emerged creature.

"Why, yes if you tell me what it is we are searching for," came the reply, simultaneously revealing a tanned skin of the face with two pairs of sickly eyes.

"That's the point," Arun remarked.

"What's the point? You don't know what we're searching for?" "Have a keen eye for some shiny object."

With the sun hiding among the hills in the clouds, the friends paused their search for the day. On his way through the jungle and into the populated part of their village, Jatin spoke up,

"So, what did your grandfather say?" "About what?"

"About this? Your new venture," "Why did he have to say anything?"

"Because... you're nine and dumb. I can see that because I am three years older,"

"What changes in three years that you have to brag about so much?" "Perhaps you will know that when you are my age," Jatin remarked savagely and went his way up the stony path to his hovel.

He was boastful but smart enough to catch his motives. Throughout the entire journey to his house, Arun was engrossed in the conversation he had with his grandfather the other day.

Seated under the shade of the cherry tree, after talking about the emergence of the cherry tree, an anecdote or two were shared about the intricacies in the way nature plays its roles in the lives of humans.

"About a hundred years ago, a faraway king, humble and noble and a great lover of cherries, on his way to an invitation planted a cherry tree here, to signify his presence and from then on, it is quite lucky to plant a cherry tree in this area,"

"Will we get juicy berries from it for the rest of our lives?"

"It may not be consistent as such but you must know the giver is always the one that gets the most, in happiness and prosperity,"

"Does the tree tell you all this?"

"No, son. If it were the case, you would've got a handful as your friends," "Did you experience it?"

"I did, we all do. When I was as tall as the money plant there, a tree saved my life,"

"Did it come to you?"

"No, but it let me hold onto its hands when I almost lost grip. That could have been a pretty nasty fall. Then to suppress my anxiety, it gave me the biggest nut there ever was and has been,"

Arun did not seem impressed then, but he was fooled enough to start on a new errand the next day. Which apparently did not go as planned.

As he glumly came through the garden door, he caught eyes with his grandpa, sunning himself in the last orange rays of the evening. His eyes were closed and held back on his hands. Arun did not say anything but presently went past the chair and into the house.

He was sad enough to have something not go his way. Yet he will not let his grandfather get in touch with that.

Even at dinnertime, he maintained his cool until grandpa sensed the lack of cheerfulness in his tone.

"What happened?" "Nothing,"

"Well, then why are you sounding as though you've got an incomplete hike?"

"What do you mean?"

Grandpa had his usual laugh at the boy's selective dumbness in particular situations, before ruffling his hair and sipping a concoction of herbs from the table.

"You are sly," Grandpa remarks, "So tell me, what have you got in mind.... some treasure?"

"Nothing, I was just off to find something in the jungle," "And what is that?"

"Something...... anything better than a nut. Shiny and crystal." "Oh, ho" Grandpa mouthed and chuckled and giggled at his grandson's profoundness and stead.

"You are quick in action, I see. But to put it bluntly, it won't help you much in the future when you are Jatin's age,"

"Why do you always have to talk about age?" "Well, Arun, you have to find that on your own," "Yes, I will find it one day, and I'll show it to you," Grandpa smiled and winked.

"And you'll be proud of me." "Oh, I am,"

The night was long and quarrelsome. Unaware of the events there was to come the next day.

A sparkle among the rustling leaves caught Arun's attention the next day. It came from beyond the bank of the stream where the water did not feed the dirt. Among the many leaves like fallen soldiers, Arun noticed a certain shine emanating from among them. White and attractive, it seemed to replicate the sun.

His friend was busy dreaming on the hard stone, so he sneaked his way towards the shine. He did notice after some time that the sparkle only showed itself from a certain angle. So after a few tries, he pinpointed the exact location, and when near, he carefully separated the rustling leaves from the object.

He must have felt that he had got his hands upon a jewel of some kind, so much so that he was pretty much in disbelief when his palms held the polished piece of glass on his palm.

"How in..." he muttered and observed the edges of it, neatly polished by the forces of water.

"So, you've found your treasure, I see," remarked a sarcastic voice from behind. Turning back, Arun sees Jatin in shorts and a sleeveless shirt, apparently waiting for his friend to make a fool of himself.

"What use does this have?" said Arun in knee-deep water.

"Everything has a purpose, that glass can be used to cut branches and char paper,"

"You seem to have the answer to everything."

"I do, but only when I think hard." Jatin said in an air of a wistful imagination.

"You don't think, you just blabber nonsense,"

“Is it? I’m not the one losing here,” Jatin remarks shrewdly, causing his friend to search for the shine in the bottom of the lake. Among the fins and swimming, the older one gets up and goes above the biggest boulder in the bank.

It was half-pressed into the dirt and the other half was placed as such to form a diving board of the stream. Jatin positioned himself like a professional, before taking off his shirt and diving into the extremes of the silky water like a sea lion or a penguin.

His friend, in the meantime, sat gloomily near the bank, contemplating his progress by viewing the glass. Presently, his friend comes to the surface triumphantly and noisily to grab his attention. In Jatin’s hand, which he places in the front above him, Arun sees a bulky river water fish flapping for dear life.

“Or perhaps you can use it to cut fish,” the fishman calmly puts out. “The list never ends for us.”

Days after his first find, Arun walks alone at midday near the stream, this time not with a blind purpose but a direction. As he heard from his grandfather, the bark of a certain tree secreted a slimy substance, which when solidified forms a gluey paste. He thought of securing it, out of desperation and the fact that he had nothing better to think about.

Schools were closed.

Jatin had gone off to another town with his uncle for work. He was pretty much on his own.

Alone and desperate for success. You could say that the hints of teenage fury and pride had surfaced in him in no time that year. Maybe it was.observing and his reasoning of things that led him to be as such: feisty and competitive.

Anyways, he had taken the long way to his reference point, observing dark-brown-coloured trees and the hint of a white paste over them. They were pretty rare yet achievable. Also, not that hard to miss.

With the prudence of the nine-year-old, one brownish-coloured tree had the hint of a white liquid dripping from off its branches. Arun was partly delighted to have found the tree, but partly confused as why he had not noticed it when it fell on his usual route to the stream.

Nonetheless, he was undeterred in claiming his find. Some of the paste which had found its way to the main stem fell on the ground below, one drop at a time.

A smear was taken from the white streak and then rubbed across the hands. Pretty sticky to hold and wood-like to smell. He decided to show it to his grandfather. If he complied with his search, he can come back for more.

Perhaps a win was waiting for him on his next visit to the place. When he had told his grandfather of the paste and argued his way into attaining it, the next day held another sly reminder of the bravery that was on display for the nine-year-old.

The finding of the paste was so celebratory for him that he didn't notice the tallness of its branches. Or of the vibrancy of its petals among the green leaves. Or of the fact that it housed a juicy and pulpy-looking fruit in its branches. One that could make a satisfying treasure for a nine-year-old.

He looked dreamily towards the tall tree, an empty bottle in his hand, stunned to move or close his mouth. The king of fruits had proved his presence and let the golden shine of the afternoon sun fall on its orange skin. It was welcoming and rewarding just to look at.

Something had powered itself again inside him and it itched to get out. Fury, it was and it caused Arun to make for the bark. Holding a certain dent edge, he let himself hold onto it and swing to another part. There he caught hold of another imperfect piece of the bark where he could secure his footing. And just like that, this climber reached the first branch, then the second, and finally onto the fringes of the third in a line.

By the time he reached the glorious branch rooting the glorious fruit, the mountains were visible from afar. Clinging from the stem at one point he made for the fruit, only to notice something else entirely.

It's the fact that he had learned climbing from his father when he was three, and although he had formidable training in climbing before he could achieve mastery in making his way back, his father disappeared.

He was not good at climbing down. And he realised that and feared that for good. All his apparent bravado was making its way through the stem and onto the hard landing below. He was a child on a tall tree. The sun too was leaving him by the minute.

Suddenly the proximity to the fruit meant nothing to him, he was choking on the summer air and he wanted to climb down. All these thoughts clouded his vision and other senses for the next minute, so much so that he didn't notice the slim figure at the bottom swinging his sun-tanned arm at him.

Even from a mile apart could he make out the signature smirk of his friend, grinning and smiling.

"Did you get it?" his friend commented.

Arun could not reply. He was paralysed with fear and embarrassment.

In the next half an hour, a lot of forceful encouragement and climbing was done on the part of both friends. When Arun did get down, it was past sundown. Yet he could visualise a set of white teeth flashing at him.

"Did you get the treasure?" "I didn't,"

"Why so?"

"It was......too tall and dangerous."

"Perhaps you got a taste of the fear. It's good for the long run." "Jatin, will you please stop saying that?"

"Ok, I'll tell you about something else."

Jatin pulled an iron chain from his back pocket and in the glow of the lights in the neighbourhood, Arun saw the piece of glass shredded into the figure of a diamond and attached to the chain.

"I got it made. You can consider it your achievement," "Why did you do that?"

"Well, I have a lengthy explanation for it. I'm sure you won't like it." Jatin replies, "Let's leave it at that."

At this point, Arun was feeling childish and dumb like his friend postulated for him. As he learned later on in his life, he was blind and ignorant towards many things. Like the fact of the treasure his grandpa had told him about.

The only way his grandfather realised it– the presence of the gift–was because he had held onto the jungle as his friend. To put it briefly, Arun would take more days to get the hang of the reality, but life had at least begun to teach him the lesson. To lift his ignorance, depicted in the respectful grin he gave back to Jatin.

This called for another remark, a closure:

Do you know what takes three years? The realisation that you have a friend. Of course, if people were to narrate this lengthy paragraph to a nine-year-old stubborn late bloomer, he would shove it away. Although, one day, someday in the future, he would remember it and smile remembering it, at the fact that how much time had passed but he didn't forget the old route into the stream, near the boulders where two friends slept fighting and searching for a treasure that stayed in their hearts for the longest time since then.